DEATH AND DISAPPEARANCES

By

Richard Smiraldi

* * * * *

Parvenue Press

* * * * *

Published in The United States of America

Parvenue Press
New York City
November 2014

For Erin, Sam, Skip, Rebecca and Margaret

Chapter One

"I don't want to talk about it," Pet said as she pushed her hair up and then let it fall to her shoulders.

"But lately Pet, we're fighting all the time and it's not like us," Mont replied.

He pulled a packet of Gitanes from his tweed wool blazer and lit a cigarette with a silver plated engraved lighter – the kind made for cigars, which featured a single flame. The lighter made a hissing sound. He puffed a bit to get the cigarette lit. He took in a deep breath of smoke and exhaled.

Pet walked over to the raised panel door of the wardrobe closet. She examined herself in a full-length mirror.

"You might've gotten me a new one. Look at it. Must we live like this? Mont, it is cracked. How long 'ave I been telling you about getting this fixed," she asked.

Mont stared out of the window and down to the street. He watched as some twenty-something's got out of a yellow taxicab, laughing. A woman fell into the arms of the man she was with. The man caught her and gently squeezed her shoulders as he helped her to stand.

"They seem so happy, so divinely happy. I wonder what that's like," he quietly asked himself.

"What were you mumbling at?" Pet asked.

He tapped the ashes outside the window and then flicked the butt towards the young lovers.

Pet looked at Mont over her shoulder as she tore open the closet door and began pulling things out and throwing them onto the floor. She yanked at sweaters and dresses and hats.

"What's all this about?" Mont asked.

"How can I go to an awards dinner looking like this? Look at me, in tares!"

"That's tears, darling, not tares."

"Stupid Mont," she muttered.

"I don't know what this obsession is with you. Nobody really cares what you look like. Look at them, the way they dress, darling –like old Hollywood. They're no one to talk."

"But you know what they say about me, Mont. What they say!"

Pet stopped when she found what she was looking for, a black Chanel cocktail dress.

She grabbed the dress and dashed into the adjoining bathroom.

"There's no rush, darling," Mont called in after her, "We've hours!"

"I know," she called through a nearly closed door.

"But Isabelle has to do my hair and makeup. I can't go looking like this, Mont. Haven't you ever had any other women in your life?"

"Yes, darling."

Mont walked over to the dressing table and picked up a tumbler he had poured earlier, half full of Scotch, and took a mouthful.

"There was my mother. But she didn't really deliberate much about where she had her hair done or how she had it done. Wasps don't do that sort of thing."

Mont could hear Pet shuffling around in the bathroom, faucet running, and smell the perfume filling the air, and hear her humming as she applied some lipstick – a nervous habit of hers he had come to love.

"You mean that nest of hornets?"

"Really, Pet, that was the style."

"The hell you say. On Mars?"

"Lissen you, 'ave an art."

"Stop mocking me."

"You know I love you, Pet."

"What's that? I can't hear you over the water running, darling."

"Never mind."

He continued drinking his Scotch and watched the traffic course down Fifth Avenue from the tenth floor window of their apartment bedroom. About an hour and forty-five minutes later his glass sat empty on an end table. He had thrown a sage-colored sofa pillow onto the floor and slid deep into an overstuffed wing chair. As he sat nearest the window some time before, he dozed off. A breeze puffed in from the street bandying about the shade in the windowsill and knocked over the Scotch tumbler. Some residual dripped to the floor.

"Wake up you. I need an honest opinion."

Mont rubbed his eyes and stretched. He looked upward at Pet as she towered over him.

The overhead light fixture beamed behind her head casting a glow about her. She looked to him like a seraph, breath-taking. Her hair was twisted into an up-do and adorned with shiny tiny jewel-type flowers. She wore long black lacy opera gloves; the Chanel cocktail dress and a violet color lip stick with a bit of rouge about her cheeks. Her eyes looked the greenest they ever had been beneath her long soft and silky lashes.

"'Ow do I luke?"

Mont looked away.

"How'd I get so lucky," he asked himself.

He looked up at her and grinned.

"Ah," she said as she fingered his lips, "that boyish smile, it gives it all away."

She giggled.

"Wait a second," he said as he moved up from his chair pressing against the arms as he did.

He reached into his blazer pocket and produced a purple velvet rectangular box.

"Oh no, Mont, you shouldn't," she said.

Mont handed the container to Pet.

Her eyes grew big as she opened it.

"Diamond earrings!"

She held her temple as her eyes flooded.

Mont rubbed his eyebrow and yawned as he glanced over at Pet.

"You fool! Now my mascara's running. I'll have to do the makeup all over again."

She tossed the box at Mont and dashed in to the bathroom and then seconds later hurried back out and snatched the article from Mont's hands.

"That's a good girl. I knew you wouldn't leave your present behind."

"I hope you didn't spend your entire advance on these."

"No, darling not all of it, just a portion."

"Now you go and get your suit."

"You mean the tuxedo?"

"You know, darling, the jacket with the silk stripes on the pants."

"Okay."

He walked out of the room with a slight jump in his step.

"She liked them. She really liked them." He smiled as he closed the bedroom door behind him. The glass doorknob turned and the latch clicked shut.

* * *

Several black limousines crowded the entrance to the club. Elderly men and women stood on line holding open the double doors to the clubhouse. Mont and Pet walked up from the corner.

"See, darling, didn't I tell you we'd make it on time. But look, there's the throng."

"The subway was definitely a capital idea, sweetheart."

He looked at Petula, "Leave it to me, darling. We don't have to wait on this line. These aren't members. The president must've opened up the event to the public. I hate when she does that."

"And why does she do this?"

"Money. Darling, it's all about money. She knows she can charge these lookie-loos a mint to get in."

"And why do they want to get in?"

"It's literary awards, darling. Everybody who's anybody is going to be here. Or at least anyone who *was* somebody will be here. Tonight they're honoring a playwright from the 1960's. He was a bit controversial. Then some famous cabaret actress will give a speech."

"And why the acteur?"

"Well, not only does it help to draw a crowd, but they're easy to find. That's an actors' club next door." Mont pointed toward the neighboring brownstone mansion.

"Over there?"

"Yes, founded by an assassin's brother."

"Let's just get inside, Mont. I'm feeling a bit chilly."

Mont grabbed hold of Petula's hand and pushed his way through the crowd, up the center staircase and to the right through a roped off section of the clubhouse marked, MEMBERS ONLY. The room was lousy with women in knee-length cocktail dresses and men in tuxedos. A waiter passed by and furnished Mont and Petula each with a glass of champagne.

"You can't see it from here, Pet, but there's a table just jam-packed with champagne glasses. They are brimming over with the stuff. And it will flow never-ending until the end of the night."

"And nobody gets drunk?"

"Not that they'll admit to. Here we just call them *tired*."

Petula tasted her glass.

"In a minute a stuffy old man will come out and ring a bell or something and tell us that we have to move to our seats. And then you shall see the parade of ancient Hollywood."

"What is this, this cavalcade you talk about old Hollywood?"

"Just a yarn we have here, me and some of the other boys. It's just that the members are all so old."

"I seem to have noticed this. But that's nice. I love to talk to the old people. They know so much."

"Is that why you go to the sketching sessions?"

"Mont, it's easier to draw people with lines."

"I know, they tell so much."

"No, silly, more texture is easier, more folds. It's the same with plump people."

Mont laughed.

"Come on, hold tight to my grip and let's find a seat."

Mont and Pet shuffled through the crowd to the back gallery. They grabbed two opera chairs nearest the aisle and sat down. She repositioned her glove, pushing the finger sleeves up her hand.

Several elderly men spoke at varying intervals. They gave speeches that seemed to tell more about their own careers and less about the literary artists they were honoring. One speaker insisted on singing his speech. He walked up to the grand piano and played a song he had written himself and sung about his merits and honors and why the club was so lucky to have him present the award.

At one point, in the middle of the song Pet leaned over and whispered into Mont's ear,

10

"Is he for real? *Sans blague?*"

Mont laughed.

"Yes, darling. He's for real. The trouble is, I don't think he realized it."

"Why do rich people always think they're like gods or something?"

"It's not that they think they're like gods. It's just that they don't know any better."

A white haired gentleman in horn-rimmed spectacles cleared his throat loudly.

"I think he's trying to tell us something," Pet said.

"Okay, darling."

The two sat up straight in their hard wooden opera seats.

After about the fifteenth chorus of "How lucky you are to be listening to me," as sung by the club man, Mont whispered,

"I think I know a way to get us out of here."

"*Vraiment?*"

"*Oui.*"

"I'll look for a break."

About forty-five minutes passed. A woman in a blue hat who sat next to Mont slowly rose from her chair.

"I have to use the facility," she whispered to her escort.

Mont stood up as well.

"I have to see to my mother," he said to the people who were sitting in front of him while he pointed at the woman who had just left.

They nodded in approval.

"She's my mother too," Pet chimed.

They hurried out the door and walked into the front parlor. A server immediately entered the room and brought them two more glasses of champagne.

Mont walked to the front of the room. Pet looked up at the vaulted stained glass ceiling.

"Is that Tiffany?"

"That's what everybody thinks. But no, it's actually designed by John La Farge."

He walked over toward the window and sat down in a chair. Pet followed him and sat in an adjacent chair.

"That really is a nice view of Gramercy Park. It's a shame it isn't public."

"Do you really believe that?"

"Why? Do you think that it's right that only select people can use the park?"

"You're such a bleeding heart."

"I don't know what that's supposed to mean, this heart, bleeding."

Mont took a sip.

"Listen, we both went to an Ivy League college, *non?*"

11

"Yes."

"Not everybody can get in, right?"

"I suppose so."

"No, you know it."

"You have to be smart."

"Or rich."

"So what does this have to do with the park?"

"That square belongs to the people who live around it. If we opened it up to the public, then anyone could go there."

"And that is wrong?"

"This isn't Europe. If we opened the park up to the public, then the public would be in there and then we couldn't be there."

"I don't understand."

"Why do you think that we spend so much of our time in private clubs?"

"I don't know. You're confusing me. In France the men go to their clubs," she laughed, "to get away from their wives, I think."

She sipped her champagne. The bubbles tingled against her lips.

She giggled.

"No seriously," he said as he took another sip of champagne.

"Darling, we come here because we're safe here."

"What do you mean by this word, **safe**?"

Mont traced his finger around the rim of the champagne glass until the crystal gave off a high pitched shrill. A server walked over.

"Mr. Clark, I'm going to have to ask you to stop doing that. You're disrupting some of the guests."

Mont looked up.

"Now Mont," Petula said as she touched his hand, "let's don't…."

"It's okay," Mont said, "I haven't had that much."

He shuffled straight in his chair and looked at the server.

"Fine, my good man. Not a problem. It won't happen again."

"Thank you," the server said and then backed away from the table and disappeared through a pair of double doors.

"I swear, Pet, I think that the servants are bigger snobs than we are."

"I am not a snob, Mont."

"You are about art."

Pet looked out of the window. She watched as a young woman walked her dog along the curb.

"I have to get back." Petula said, suddenly.

"Why?" he asked, puzzled.

"The dog! I have to walk Mrs. Hamilton."

Thoughts whirled around his brain. He was confused. He remembered that they had lost the dog earlier that afternoon. She escaped through an open door. Pet must have forgotten. He decided *not* to remind her.

"Okay, darling. Let's wait until the intermission or whenever the old boys break up. There are a few people I promised mother I'd give her regards to. We can leave but let's not make a social *faux pas*. I need for this next book to do well, so that we can do some of the things we talked about."

"You mean, *Mont Martre?*"

"That too, darling."

"How is it that your father doesn't release the funds?"

"Not here, darling. We can discuss this later."

She looked out into the bar and could spot one or two figures in the sculpture garden.

"That's what he always says, but he never does. No, we don't talk about it," she said, talking to herself.

"The male mind, I don't think I ever understand it. But I love him, that silly writer boy."

She pressed her eyes closed and tapped her heart.

The doors to the back gallery opened. The sounds of voices chattering filled the entry rooms as the crowd made their way in to the parlor where Montgomery and Petula were seated. A woman in a puffy-sleeved ball gown walked over to Mont and tapped his shoulder.

"I hope I haven't woken you," she said.

"Oh missus…" He paused for a moment trying to remember."

"It's Linda Rutledge, from Upper Montclair."

"Oh, hi, Mrs.… er… um, Linda."

A man in a well-tailored black suit and silver bow tie moved forward and extended his hand.

"This is Steve Mikalski."

"Your husband?"

Linda laughed.

"Not yet. Maybe if he's lucky. He's my agent." Her eyes scanned the parlor.

"Oh."

Linda flashed him a smile. She pursed her lips.

"She knows damned well that I play for the other team," Steve joked. He patted Mont on the back and extended his hand. Mont half-rose from his seat. He tickled the palm of Mont's hand as they shook. Disgusted Mont pulled his hand back and self-consciously wiped his sleeve as he sat back down. Steve studied the pattern of the Persian carpeting, half-smirking and feigning shame.

Steve glanced upwardly. His gaze caught Mont's. They eyed one another and steamed off a collective chuckle, the kind of boarding school locker room chortles that men share when breaching uncomfortable stations.

Petula opened her eyes. She sensed Mont's uneasiness.

"The other team?" Her eyes narrowed at Steve. "Are you in the sports?"

They all laughed nervously.

"And who is this vision?" Steve asked, recovering his face.

Mont grinned. He flashed a sparkle at his wife.

"I think he's in love," Linda remarked, playfully.

Petula removed her hand from Mont.

"More than that." He took Pet's hand in his. "This is my wife. May I present to you Mrs. Petula Beaujolais-Clark." He did a funny thing with his hand as he said this, as if he were presenting Royalty waving his hand above his head and spiraling downward.

Pet's cheek's turned a rosy color. Her dimples were illuminated in the moonlight that shone through the windows.

"Well that's a mouthful, I must say," Linda added.

"I don't mind. It comes with the territory," she said as she squeezed his hand and whispered something in his ear. He couldn't understand what she had said but nodded and smiled as the champagne from her breath wet his ear.

"Please tell your father, Mont, that we are behind him one hundred percent, and also give my regards to your mother."

"Will do," Mont said as he rubbed his ear lobe.

Linda took Steve's arm and the couple nodded and then turned and walked back into the parlor.

"What did she mean by that," Pet asked.

"By what?"

"About your father?"

"I don't know. Honestly. I haven't spoken to my parents since Christmas. They've been traveling."

"And Easter?"

"Well you remember we sent flowers," she said.

He raised an eyebrow. "Didn't we send roses or something?"

"I don't know. I'm not remembering," she said as she rubbed at her temple.

"You know Pet; this is the trouble with two artists married together."

"I know the painter, me," she pointed to herself, "and the writer, you," she pointed to Mont.

"And not an ounce of common sense between us," he said.

They laughed.

"I think we did have the florist to send some flowers. I'll have to check in the desk. But I'm sure of it because I sent something to ma Grandmère. I did it at the same time."

"That's a relief. They hate us as it is."

"What do you mean by this word, hate?"

"You get it, Pet."

"Oh, about the wedding?"

"Yes. You know how mother is."

14

"No, that's just the problem. If you'd let me go up there and spend some time, maybe I could win her over."

Mont took a sip of his flat champagne and then spit it back into the glass.

"Isn't it strange, Pet? When you first get here, they can't give you enough fresh champagne. But the minute the event is over, all the champagne goes flat."

"And why is that?"

"I think it's because they want us to get the harder stuff and sign for it at the bar."

"Harder?"

"You know, Scotch or Gin or…" he smiled at her, "what's that you like so much?"

"Veuve Clicquot."

"Right."

"And it's dear."

"Trés dear, darling."

"Right. It's how they make the money."

"I suppose."

Another couple came up to Mont and Pet. The man was in a Military uniform.

"Really, let's go," she whispered in to his ear like a little girl.

"I'm sorry, General Peterson," he looked over at his wife and clutched her arm in his, "we'll have to beg off, my wife has developed this terrible headache." They rose from their chairs.

The General nodded.

Pet tapped at her temple with her index finger.

"Best to get her home and take care of her, young man."

"Yes, sir."

Mont put his arm around Petula and walked her down the stairs, out the door and into a taxi, which had been waiting outside for a fare.

Chapter Two

"Did I wake you?"

"Zawamba in high heaven! Who is this?"

"I'm sorry, I'll call back."

"No, dear boy. You've already got me on the line at..." she paused.

Her hands fumbled around in the dark, out from under her 800 count Egyptian cotton sheets and over towards the nightstand. A few items crashed to the floor. Something broke. She reached over and fumbled finally finding a cylindrical object with ears - her night owl clock. She held it up in front of her eyes that were covered by a night mask. She smacked the side of her head with her hand and then lifted the mask and looked at the clock.

"4-A-M! You've gotten me up at 4-A-M! This better be good, M, or I swear..."

He interrupted her.

"She left me again."

The line went quiet. Beatrice could hear him breathing heavily on the other end as he sniffled intermittently.

"This is really bad," she thought to herself.

"Where are you, darling? Are you in a safe place?"

"I'm okay. Don't worry."

"No, listen to me...." Beatrice said, as she gripped the phone mouthpiece closer to her lips, "are you safe?"

He laughed nervously.

"I'm in my Scooby-Doo pajamas sitting Indian style on my bed with a cup of hot cocoa beside me. Now how more safe can I be?"

"Say, there isn't anything *in* that cocoa, is there," she asked, half-jokingly and attempting at some levity.

"Just cocoa, honest," he said, as he crossed his heart with his fingers.

"That's something she taught me, something she used to do," he thought to himself. He got teary-eyed, and wiped his eyes on his left pajama sleeve.

"Honestly, Bea, I swear on Methuselah's grave," he said, his voice a bit hoarse.

Bea ripped the mask from her forehead and threw it across the room. Her head had begun to pound. The mask knocked something off a table. The sound of the objects hitting the floor roared into the phone. Mont half-smiled.

"Good old Bea," he thought.

"I don't know if I believe you. Did you just swear on your dead goldfish's grave?"

"Yes and he was *your* fish if you remember correctly."

"That's *not* the point and besides, there's something I've been meaning to ask you."

"And?"

Beatrice repositioned the pillow behind her head.

"How exactly can you tell the sex of a goldfish?"

Static blared through the phone. She banged the receiver on the nightstand a few times. The feedback dissolved.

"Damned Bakelite. I've been meaning to get this thing repaired," she said. He cleared his throat.

"She left me. This time I think that it's for good."

"Now, darling, let's not get upset. We've been through this all before."

"I feel numb; like I'm fading and queasy, Bea. My fingertips are tingling."

"Now don't let's panic, darling. I'll round up some of the gang and we'll scout out her usual haunts."

"At 4 o'clock? You *are* a good friend."

"It's 4:15, darling…"

The line fell silent. He could hear Beatrice nervously tapping on the other end of the phone with her index finger.

"Mont, can you tell me what she was wearing?"

"I'll try. Give me a second, the head, it hurts."

Mont reached over to the nightstand and picked up a bottle of aspirin. He gulped down two pills and followed them with a sip of water. His eyes raced around the room. He focused on the closet door. He could see the sleeve of one of her party dresses as it poked through the darkness.

"A slip, a sable coat – champagne color, and a pair of fuzzy pink slippers."

"That's how she left you?"

"We quarreled."

"It must've been some helluva fight!"

Mont began to sob.

"Honestly, darling, we'll find her. I mean, it's a tiny island, how far could she go?"

He cleared his throat. He had some trouble swallowing. The aspirin was lodged. He took another sip of water.

"It's thirteen miles long," he answered.

"What," she asked, confused.

"Manhattan; its thirteen miles long."

"Oh," Beatrice replied.

He rubbed his nose with his sleeve and repositioned the telephone against his ear. His eyes and nose burned.

"Listen doll, let me whip up this body into some semblance of order and call around. I will ring you back in twenty minutes."

"Okay."

"And for Pete's sake, Mont, stay away from those open windows."

* * *

18

The ride to the New York Public Library on Fifth Avenue felt longer than usual.

The train jostled up and down and stalled at Fifty-eighth Street. Mont knew he could get out at Fifty-seventh and walk down, but it was cold and he was only wearing his tweed jacket and thought it better to ride the train to Grand Central Station.

"I'll go to the big library with the lions," he thought. "I'll go there every day for the rest of my life. I will go until this pain stops hurting. How the hell am I supposed to write," he looked up and asked a picture of a man in an advertisement for underwear.

He clutched at his messenger bag strap.

"She knows I do this. She knows where to find me."

A couple seated across from him on the subway looked with disdain over at him mumbling to himself. He covered his mouth with his hand.

"Oh I didn't want get out of bed this morning," he thought to himself, "or any morning since that first one. What I want is to stay in our apartment. But if I do that ..." The exit bell to the train bleeped and disrupted his thoughts. The doors slid open.

Mont stumbled out of the train as the crowd pushed behind him. He wandered forward to the stairwell. A woman uttered something disparaging at him as he grasped onto the rail and rode the escalator up to the main floor. He squinted. The fluorescent lights overhead seemed brighter than usual and burned his eyes.

"Cold, heartless motherfckin' city," he thought.

People hurried by him holding briefcases, newspapers and coffee. They rushed to their offices, their places of work, going through the motions of their daily routines. They moved like a sea of tropical fish in a rhythm all seemingly keeping time, in step, like a great orchestra of performers, knowing where they were going, what they were doing and what their part on this planet was.

"Somebody please tell me that this isn't my life. This can't be happening to me," he cried, but no one seemed to notice.

Mont stood still for awhile in the center of Grand Central Station by the circular information stand and watched as people: men, women, children, tourists, cabbies, vendors, shop-keeps, businessmen all rushed by. All of humanity seemingly made their way around him, passing him as if he were invisible and not really there at all, like a log caught against a rock amidst a burbling river.

He watched as he attempted at hurrying with the crowd up the western ramp to the outdoors. A parade of umbrellas marched passed on the sidewalk outside.

"Great, it's raining and I've no umbrella! Figures!" he said as he clutched his tweed jacket lapel closed and squeezed his messenger bag strap.

He ran up the ramp and out the doors nearly knocking over a Chinese Food delivery boy on a bicycle whizzing past.

"Watch it, bro!" A man selling hats and scarves yelled at him.

Mont crossed the street and hurried to Madison Avenue down the block and corner. He got caught at the traffic light. Its red hue looked blurry amidst the rain.

The streets wafted the odor of wet newspapers, cigarette butts, coffee, praline nuts, and exhaust fumes from the traffic as it hummed and honked by.

Mont was drenched with rain and feeling a bit chilly and feverish. He sneezed into his fist.

A bus zoomed past on 42nd Street, hit a puddle and splashed him. Chills ran up and down his spine.

"Great, just great!" he cried. He sneezed again.

Hurrying, he ran across the street and up the stairs of the New York Public Library nearly slipping and falling down the marble steps. The library felt warm and dry. He walked into the reading room.

After about three hours of sitting with only one word written on his yellow legal pad: FORLORN, he slid the pad into his messenger bag. He got up and walked quietly across the marble floor passing rows of reading tables out through the foyer, then the front door and finally down the stairs to the front sidewalk bordering Fifth Avenue.

"This is just a waste of time - an effort in futility. I can't write. How can my publisher expect me to write when I'm so shook up?"

Just then a woman clad in a big feather hat and fashionable haute couture outfit appeared before him.

"Monty, as I live and breathe!"

The rain had stopped. Mont smiled at her.

"Figures, Bea, you come along and suddenly it's sunny."

" I bet you say that to all the girls."

"Girl?"

"Watch it kid or I'll slap you."

She walked over to him.

"Come, darling, give us a big hug!" She held her arms out wide, big and theatrical while holding on to her handbag.

He went to hug her.

"Careful, darling, you'll crush the…"

Bea looked down at the gardenia on her lapel,

"Well whatever this is," she said as she smiled.

He feigned a hug, but didn't get too close.

"I've come, darling, to take you to lunch."

"Where?"

"As if you have to ask. It's Thursday."

"Oh that's right, I'd nearly forgotten, 21."

"I should smack you. You really are out of sorts."

They walked arm and arm in to the limo and rode up to 21 West 52nd Street. The driver stopped the limousine, exited, walked around the back of the car and opened the door. As the chauffer opened the door, the doorman peeked in and greeted Beatrice, taking his hat off to her.

"They're too kind, aren't they just? Acting like I'm actually somebody."

"Aren't you?"

"Oh, you know what I mean," she said as she tapped his arm playfully.

They walked past the doorman in to the restaurant.

"I need to stop off at the little writer's room and I'll be right back."

"You know, there are writers who are women, I don't really like you calling it that. You've developed a few new traits, I have to say, that I'm not at all too fond of."

He stepped down in to the men's room. As he opened the restroom door, he could hear the races playing on the attendant's portable radio. Beatrice walked down the stairs toward the restaurant/bar area.

About fifteen minutes had past. Mont exited the restroom and entered the back dining room; he passed tables full of chattering businessmen and women of every variety with too many teeth, either talking to each other or with cell phones seemingly glued to their ears. He nudged by waiters and busboys with their sweaty brows, and felt uneasy. Mont hated crowded rooms.

There in the distance he spotted Bea's hat feather. With Bea there was always a big hat, something loud and outrageous. (Her hats were notorious. The local shops had made her something of a second rate celebrity, an icon of hatters everywhere). This hat had a green Ostrich plume, which dusted the toy truck that was strung from the ceiling directly above her. The feather bobbed when either she exaggerated her walk along the tile floor-way or when she spoke, if she were overly engrossed in the topic or feigning the same – which was more likely the case – a bobble with every syllable she emphasized.

Mont pulled out a chair at the table.

"I'd have preferred to be upstairs, darling, but you know how it is with the way they're seating everybody these days. Like we're King and Queen something or other, side by side. I mean, it's one thing if the fella is," she paused for a moment and shrugged her shoulders as her feather tapped the truck, "your fella, but, darling, it's quite another when it's just friends. I'm sure it must be the chef's idea - you know, so that we pay more attention to the food and less to each other. But really, darling, it's 21, is all that necessary?"

He looked at her as he lowered himself into the seat.

"It has been awhile, hasn't it?" he asked.

She waved her linen napkin in the air as if she were surrendering. A waiter in the corner spotted her and rushed over with menus. He put an oversized fold in front of each of them.

Mont glanced at Beatrice.

"I don't even need to look, I'll just have a hamburger and coffee," he said to the hovering waiter who scribbled it down. Mont folded the menu closed and handed it back to the waiter. The waiter slipped the menu tightly under his arm.

"Really, darling? Honestly! Who comes to 21 for just a hamburger? Do they even serve burgers? No, sweetheart, I insist that you order something else."

"But I'm not hungry, it would just be a waste."

"Darling, you need sustenance."

"Okay," he muttered.

"I'll have the chicken and whatever comes with it." The waiter scratched into the pad and wrote down the new order.

"Very good, sir," the waiter replied. He nervously looked at Beatrice, "And for you Miss?"

"You call me *Miss*, ah *garçon*, you do flatter me," she said as she smiled coyly into her menu and fingered her gardenia.

"Waiter, I'll have *Le Duc L'Orange*," she said, over-emphasizing her accent.

The waiter looked at her bewildered.

"Well what's wrong, Frenchy? Go get me some duck," she clamored as she waved her hand shooing the waiter.

As she folded the menu flat and handed it to the waiter she turned toward Mont.

"Oh brother, here comes the performance," he thought.

"I'll tell you, they should really hire some help that understand English. Look at him. He stares at me like I'm speaking Portuguese."

The waiter cleared his throat.

"Miss, I speak the English just fine."

"Then what's the trouble?"

"The trouble is," the waiter said somewhat frustrated, "is that we do not a serve the duck at this establishment today!"

"Oh my heavens, no need to get so hot around the collar," she said as she rubbed the back of her neck.

Taking the menu back into her hands, she opened it, scanned down the specials, quickly glanced up and down the fold.

"Then just bring me the lamb with mint sauce," she blurted out, her voice quivering.

Mont shuffled in his seat, uncomfortable.

"It's Thursday. I always have the lamb on Thursdays, it does something for me," she tapped her chest, "gives me the strength to shop. Shopping can be quite exhausting, darling!"

The waiter stood, unmoved.

Bea smirked.

"What is it now, Frenchy?"

"I'm sorry, Miss, but there is no lamb. It isn't in the menu. You need to order from the menu."

With her eyes she traced the clef in Mont's chin.

"Alright, then," she smiled, "just bring me a Cobb salad. We'll let this go for today. You can manage that now, can't you," she said in a bass tone she reserved for servants and others whom she believed were inferior to her.

"Very good, Madam," the waiter replied. He hurried from the table, pushed a chair from the row in, and then disappeared into a crowded aisle and through the door to the kitchen.

Opening a compact from her purse, she peered into the tiny mirror and examined her makeup. Taking the cotton pad, she dabbed some powder on to her nose and then snapped it shut and deposited it. She placed the purse on the floor to her side while wrapping the shoulder strap around her ankle.

They sat in silence for a few minutes. He spotted a fly as it landed on the toy truck above Beatrice's head. His eyes wandered around the room. In the far corner, almost with some predictability, he noticed a chubby, open-faced man in a poly-blend suit – the kind one finds on the racks at discount department stores. The sleeves were a bit too short for the salesman's chubby arms. The man wore a dingy fedora on his head and clenched an unlit cigar between his fingers. He was talking to a younger woman. Her hair was tinted platinum blonde. She giggled an infectious laugh and seemed to be peeking around as if trying desperately to hold on to a secret.

"That one there's a better-offer type," Bea remarked after having watched Mont eyeing the woman.

"What do you mean?"

"Well, you see who she's with? That man can't be anyone, or if he is, let's just say he hides it well."

"I'm not sure I know what you're getting at." Mont said.

"Better offer; she's looking for a better offer. This guy is thinking here he's the big cheese. He's probably a sales type or something like it, and there she is, getting the free meal, while he thinks everyone is wondering how he ended up with a gal like that. But she is on the hunt for a better offer, you know, somebody who can do more for her."

"Oh Bea, things like that don't go on anymore. You're just imagining it."

"I wouldn't be so smug, Mont. She just looked over at you."

"Nonsense. It could be that the man she is with is a relative, a father, or Uncle or something who's taking his college-aged niece out for lunch."

"Oh he's her Uncle alright. I've had a few of those 'Uncles' myself, not that I'm too proud. But don't carry on in 21. Not here!"

"Now I've heard everything. Why is it with you that everything's a drama?"

23

"I can't say that I know what you're talking about," she said as she smiled coyly.

A few minutes passed. Beatrice examined the room as if she were searching for something or someone.

The waiter came with a young server behind him carrying two tray stand and plates of food. They promptly placed the steaming dish of chicken in front of Mont and the Cobb salad before Beatrice and hurried off. Another server came and with silver tongs placed bread on the smallest dishes. Beatrice nodded with approval.

"At last, we dine!" Mont announced ceremoniously. What?" He said looking at her. "You're not the only actor in the house, can't I have some fun too?" Beatrice looked at him disapprovingly.

He heard his stomach growl. Before long his plate was clean, while Beatrice slowly chewed her salad, somewhat reluctantly.

"I say, you've gone through that, like Grant took Richmond while I feel like I'm grazing."

"Bessie," Mont laughed. He smiled and sipped some water and dotted his mouth with his napkin.

"I hadn't of realized how hungry I was. I guess I haven't been eating since she left."

"That certainly says something."

"You saved me, Bea. I nearly would've starved to death if you didn't appear as you did. How'd you know I'd be at the library?"

"Darling, I didn't know anything! Naturally at that hour of the day I'm on Fifth Avenue. It's where I shop. It was just a happy coincidence that I met up with you. As for luncheon, doll, when it comes to Thursday, you can always count on me for 21."

Beatrice pushed her barely touched Cobb salad aside. She called the waiter over and ordered a glass of Chardonnay.

The waiter promptly returned with the wine. A busboy followed and removed her salad plate. Bea held the glass up to her nose, took a whiff and smiled. Swirling it around she held it to the light. Once she was satisfied with what she saw, she very slowly took a sip, held it in her mouth, gave a closed mouth smile and swallowed. Mont ordered a coffee. Within seconds the cup and saucer appeared.

"That was fast!" he said as he picked up the black coffee.

"You know, I feel like I'm drinking alone."

"Why, because I'm not imbibing?" he said as he took a sip.

"In a manner of speaking, yes!"

"Please Bea. I don't drink when I'm un (he paused) happy. It only makes matters worse."

"Do you always do that?"

"What?"

"Not that I never noticed before, but when you say the word unhappy?"

"Yes, what?"

"You sort of pause between un and happy."

"I do?"

"Yes."

"I hadn't noticed."

"Say it again."

"Please, Bea, you're making me blush."

"Say it, Puritan!"

"Alright then," he said.

He nudged the coffee cup saucer and said, "un (pause) happy."

"See, you're doing it. I knew it couldn't be the wine going to my head!"

"I guess I do. I guess we all do. It's probably..." his voice trailed off.

"Don't think about her."

"It's hard not to."

Bea's eyes circled. She looked at one of the Remington drawings hanging on a post.

"See that drawing over there,"

"Where?"

"That one," she pointed, "has a picture of a man with some kind of still in front of him, and corn liquor or something, probably done during Prohibition. I always say that - that one is of me! He's asking the waiter for ice!"

"Why because you're a difficult patron," Mont said, jokingly.

"Let's just say I require *extra* service."

They both laughed. Bea noticed that the blonde had gone. The man in the cheap suit was preoccupied with a cell phone call.

Some Texan tourists with big hair and too much perfume knocked into the table as the passed by.

"I'll never get used to this," Beatrice said.

"What?"

"The way they march in here like elephants in the Big Top."

"Please, Bea. If you don't like the tourist trade, why do you come? You know this is one of the spots. They visit to gaze at all the gadgets hanging from the ceiling."

Beatrice looked up.

"Quite a menagerie, I'd say."

"Advertising props."

"I know I heard all about the time when Howard Hughes hung that plane over there to impress a client."

"But listen, there are also cardboard boxes and football helmets hanging from the ceiling! I mean at these prices you'd think..."

"Don't say it, I won't have you tell me anything bad about 21."

"What is it, sacrosanct?"

"Careful or the gods will knock one of those items down on that pretty little head of yours."

"And kill me? I don't think so. The chains that hold them up look pretty sturdy, Bea."

A large woman with enormous hair bumped up against the table.

"Sorry ma'am, sir," she said as she brushed by clutching her bag to her side.

"See what I mean about these tourists? I don't see why I shouldn't come here when I was here first."

"What do you mean by that? First? How old are you exactly, Bea? You were first at 21? Why that'd make you…" He paused.

"Watch it."

She pulled a tube from her purse and reapplied her lipstick, then took a napkin and blotted her lips.

"She does this at the table," he thought, "she didn't learn that at Miss Porters."

"I only meant that I got here before them. And quite frankly, for Texans, I thought they might be a little bit lighter on their feet. And just look at their faces."

"What, darling?"

"Have you ever noticed how the face is a different color than the neck? It's like the woman's face is on a pedestal, displayed."

"That's deliberate, darling. It goes with the hair. Besides, I love Texan women, the accent, the way they walk, the confidence, the ardor, and the glam. They just don't roll out of bed. They spend hours getting themselves all dollied up — Neiman Marcus or something. It's just wonderful. I love a gal who fusses," he said mocking Bea, "it just does something for me."

"Well you don't really, darling. Do you," Bea asked.

"Now what do you mean by that?" he asked as he leaned towards her.

"Well you know we have to have this conversation."

"No, we don't."

"Yes we do. It's eating you up."

"Maybe just around the edges, but careful cougar."

"Darling, it's killing you. You might as well tell me here."

"Here, at 21 with these big-mopped Rodeo clowns?"

"A moment ago you were reveling in their ardor."

"In public, Bea. Really?"

"We're always in public, darling."

"Well I told you she left me. She left in the middle of the night."

"It was in the wee hours that you telephoned."

"Whatever."

"And in a sable coat and slippers?"

"That's correct."

"No literary license there?"

"None."

"So the little French girl leaves you in the middle of the night. And you can't eat or sleep for days. You wake up all of your friends, not that we mind. You have us call all over and search and try, try, try, to find the little mouse, and maybe, you know where she is all along?"

"I don't, Bea. Honest."

"And she hasn't been back to the flat to collect her things?"

"I don't know. I mean, I don't think so."

"It doesn't surprise me."

"Now what's that supposed to mean?"

Mont leaned back and took a drink of his water. He reached into his pocket for his Gitanes, grabbed the box and then let it slip back into his jacket, realizing that he couldn't smoke there.

"I know; I'm dying for a fag myself. The trouble is, none of these bars let you anymore, and they don't care who you are or what ship your family came in on," Beatrice said, as she flashed a phony smile at a passing waiter.

"Listen," she leaned forward and put her hand on his knee. Mont grabbed her hand and immediately threw it off of him and toward the floor. He looked around the room. Bea leaned back.

"Goodness," she said, a bit embarrassed by his last action, "she's not like us."

"Now what the hell is that supposed to mean, not like us? She breathes the same air. Her heart beats. She gets up every day, eats, showers, craps…she's human. Petula is like us, Bea."

"Sometimes I think you're just a miracle of deafness. Don't be such a simpleton."

"Well, I've been called many things in my life, Bea, but that is not one of them."

"Okay, so I take it back, the simple part. But listen, sweetie, when it comes to Petula, well it's like you've got your blinders on. I mean, you don't see a thing when it's staring you right there in the eyes, plain and foreign."

"Okay, so now you're xenophobic?"

"Oh my Heavenly days," Bea cried, "my last husband, Laszlo, was a Hungarian, and honey; you don't get much more exotic than that. What I'm trying to say is this…"

She stopped talking. Clenching the stem of her glass, she raised it up slowly, as if to make a toast.

"Oh, waiter," she said barely audible, in a very dry voice.

"Yes," a nervous thin man in checkered pants and an apron answered (he's been looming around the table – but on Beatrice patrol).

"There's a problem with my glass."

"What is it?" he said as he wiped his clammy hands on his apron.

"There's a hole in it."

The waiter looked at her somewhat confused.

"It's empty, darling!"

She motioned to the waiter to bring her another glass. The waiter grimaced and then dashed to the bar. Within seconds he brought over another glass of wine and placed a cocktail napkin down and then gently rested the wine glass on top of it. Bea nodded in approval. She smiled. This time Bea raised her glass, holding it by the stem with her pinky extended, as the waiter took the empty glass away, she took a sip and toasted,

"Nectar of the gods! Bottoms up!"

"And that's big bottoms to you, darling!"

She laughed. "Big bottoms! How about big bottoms and bigger bosoms," she cackled.

"When you do that, you sound almost like Elizabeth Taylor. Really, I think you're becoming a bit of a lush."

"Becoming? I'd say I've earned the title by now. You've got to admit, I've been working up to it for some time. Five husbands! Do you have any idea what it's like to be a woman my age with five divorces under her belt? I must say, around these parts, that I'm like that black widow – except none of them are dead," she paused for dramatic effect and then continued, "just their bank accounts…. and was that old Elizabeth – Who's Afraid of Virginia Woolf Elizabeth, or Father of the Bride, Elizabeth?"

"Oh, Bea, you're silly, I wasn't serious," Mont said. "And didn't the first husband die?" He tapped her hand.

"Oh, right, Alger. Yes, Alger has been laid to rest. But if you ask me, his breath died ten years before he did!" She made a drum sound on the table, "ba dum dum" she said and let out a giant laugh. A few of the Texans from a neighboring table looked over, annoyed.

Beatrice wiped her mouth on her sleeve.

"Let's get off me, shall we, and back on to you. I mean you're the one that can't sleep or write. And quite frankly, I'm worried about you. In all the years I have known you, I've never seen you like this," she said, genuinely. He grimaced.

"Don't worry about me. Petula will come back, she always does."

"That's just it. She leaves you in a huff after some little spat and then you take her back, that girl of yours."

"Bea, she isn't a girl."

"What do you mean?"

"She's my wife, Bea. I married her."

"Do you mean to tell me that all that business was actually true?"

"I married her while we were still at Columbia University. You know this."

"Yes, but I didn't believe it. I mean it's not like you *had* to or anything?"

Mont turned away from the table toward the back of the room. He didn't say anything.

"Now I've gone and upset you."

She looked toward the bar as she fidgeted with her linen napkin.

"Look at me."

Mont continued to look away.

"Look, whatever it was I said, I am sorry. I didn't think. I have a big mouth and I always put my foot in it."

Mont glanced over at her and then away.

"That's the trouble with you, Bea, you never think, he said to the wall."

"Whatever it was that you thought I meant, I'm sure you took it the wrong way."

"Did I, Bea," he replied back at her.

Bea called the waiter, "Garcon, bring this boy a Chardonnay."

Mont looked up.

"Make it a Scotch, neat," he answered.

Bea smiled. Mont forced a fake smile, mimicking her.

"That's my boy."

"I'm not your *boy*. The truth is, I'm not anybody's boy, at least not anymore. It doesn't feel that way."

"This is serious."

A busboy came up to the table with a sterling silver crumb sweeper and brushed the table. Bea lifted her glass so that the boy could clear the checkered tablecloth. Mont rested his elbow on the table. He did not move. The waiter appeared carrying a tumbler of Scotch. A rind of lemon floated near the top. He placed the glass down in front of Mont and alongside it a small bowl of mixed nuts and a tiny crystal pitcher of water and a water glass.

"I said neat, waiter."

"I know you did, sir, but it is customary to bring the water even if you never drink it," he winked.

"Okay, you can leave it," Mont said.

He waved the waiter away with his hand and then held his head with it.

"What, do you have a headache?"

Mont put his hand down.

"No. It's just all this serious talk. It's a bit much to take."

"Can we dispense with the dramatics? Really, darling, that's **my** department."

Mont forced a laugh.

"You always know how to distract me, even in the midst of this."

Beatrice readjusted her hat, fixing the pins.

"Don't you remember that time at the fountain outside The Plaza?" she said.

"You and what were they…" he mused.

"Shriners, darling."

"Are you sure?"

"Well they had to be, with all those funny little hats?"

"But how'd they get you into that negligee?"

Beatrice burst out laughing. She nearly knocked over her glass of wine.

"I was doing a fashion shoot, darling, for a lingerie company. Honestly, Mont, the things you get into that silly little head of yours."

"I know I didn't imagine it."

Beatrice dabbed at her face with her napkin. Mont took a healthy sip of his Scotch. It felt warm as it trickled down his throat.

"You see; this is what you need to be doing."

He smiled.

"You need to be having lunch with very old friends."

"Very *old* friends," he laughed.

"Watch it!"

She took a sip of her wine.

"And having wine and laughing and enjoying yourself. You can't just wallow away in that apartment sulking."

"I was at the library."

"Who cares where you were, you weren't happy, darling."

"Can you blame me?"

"I know it's rough. But heartache and I, we're old friends, dear, and it never gets any easier." she said as she patted her gardenia.

"Doesn't it?"

"Only if you make yourself hard."

Mont laughed.

"And who wants that," they said at the same time, laughing.

"You know, sometimes I wish I could make you small and carry you around in my pocket to make me laugh when I'm feeling low."

She blushed.

"Stop. You'll make me cry."

"Hard old Bea cry? Please."

"Can we stop with the 'old,' I mean, seriously, I'm not much older than you."

"Much."

"Can we get back to the issue at hand?"

"What?"

"The girl."

"My wife?"

"Okay then, your wife."

"You were saying how she wasn't *one of us*."

"Well how did you meet her anyway?"

"You know the story."

"No, I don't really. I mean, you never did tell me. I heard from our friends, at the club. A little here, a little there, but never the out and out bit. So maybe it will help you if you spit it out."

"It's like pulling a rusty dagger from my heart." He pantomimed the action.

"You know, that's really good. Maybe you could use it in something you're writing?"

"That's just the trouble, I'm not. I'm not writing."

She wiped her eyelid.

"Okay, well have another sip, or five, and then tell me."

He motioned a military salute to her, smiled and gulped about two thirds of the tumbler of Scotch down.

"I must say I *am* impressed."

"Well it's not like I didn't go to the parties at St. A's."

"Yes, I've heard stories about that frat."

"Yes, those were happy times at Columbia, filled with rife. But it's hard for me to think about it anymore."

"It might do you some good to have a purge."

"The way you say *purge*, it almost sounds like something naughty."

"Well maybe that's just how I mean it. Now spill!"

"So that's where I met her. She was studying art at Barnard. This might surprise you, but Pet was a *Barnard* girl."

"It doesn't surprise me at all. They let lots of people in."

"She deserved to be there, honest she did."

"So you had some classes with her, core no doubt."

"No, that's not how I met her. I was studying English, we call it reading letters."

"And what was the little wraith's major?"

"Can we please refrain from the insults? You don't know how it pains me." He rubbed his chest with his hand.

"Oh I am sorry, dear boy."

"I know it," he said as he patted her padded shoulder, "catty is your nature."

"Ouch, but true," she said as she smiled back at him. "Go on. Stop deflecting."

"Okay, where was I?" He finished his Scotch.

A waiter came to the table and brought him a fresh glass. He pushed the empty tumbler to the edge of the table and the waiter took it away while Bea nursed her drink.

"I'll tell you the way that I met her. It was all on account of Peter."

"Peter?"

"You remember, he was my roommate at school."

"Oh that's right. Wasn't he…?" Her voice trailed off.

"What?"

"Well for lack of a better word Mont, superfluous?"

"You mean homosexual?"

"Well yes? Wasn't he gay?"

"I don't see why that matters."

"Well I think, dear boy, that it matters a great deal. It helps me to put things into perspective."

"Well, darling, I have to say, that's a bridge that we never crossed."

"I've had my doubts."

"Can I get on with the story?"

"Yes, Mont, do go on."

"Well there I was, in the middle of the fall term. As you well know, I kept a journal then. I wrote in it every day."

"You know what they say about journals, darling."

"I know, that people without lives write about them."

"Yes."

"But I don't think that applies to writers, Bea, I mean, that's what we do, write."

"Okay, well just get on with it then. You were where?"

"I was in the quad. Peter had stolen my journal and I was feverishly chasing him across the quad to get it back. "

He looked up as if to see if anyone were eavesdropping and then looked back at Bea.

"Don't worry, darling, no reporters, I checked when I came in."

"Well anyway there I was chasing after his skinny swimmer's ass. I was terrified. I wrote about everyone and everything and more importantly how I truly felt about them."

"Did you ever think he'd stolen the book to find out how you felt about him and his skinny swimmer's ass?"

"He wouldn't have discovered very much. I rarely thought about him. I just sort of took him for granted. He was a good roommate and a better friend."

"Or so you thought."

"No I still think in all fairness that he was a good friend, I mean is a good friend. He's not dead."

"And so Peter stole your journal and you two were skipping across the quad?"

"I was running, Bea. Leave the literary license to me, eh?"

"Okay."

"So I chased him and I wasn't paying attention to where I was going."

"You rarely are."

"And I accidentally tripped over Petula."

"She was there in the quad?"

"On a bicycle no less. One of those antique lady's jobs."

"And so that was your meet cute?"

"Not exactly. I mean she was furious with me."

"Now I'm intrigued. Why was the little snipe angry with you?"

"Apparently she was taking her final painting, an expressionist piece done in acrylics, to be juried for a final grade."

"And?"

"In my haste to get my journal back, I knocked her over and my foot…"

He looked down at his left foot and held it up.

"You didn't?"

"I did, right through her canvas. The piece was ruined."

"Young love."

"Not so fast," he said as he started to cry.

"Oh Mont," she said. She handed him her linen napkin. He took it from her hand and dabbed his eyes.

"I'm sorry. It just gets to me, you know?"

"Yes, darling. Have some more medicine," Bea said as she slid the Scotch over toward him.

Mont took another gulp. He swallowed hard and wiped his nose with the napkin.

Bea took the napkin from Mont and held it in the air until a waiter came by and retrieved it and gave her a fresh one.

"I'll never forget the look that she gave me, like a mad bull. She turned beet read, and her cheeks were going in and out. She was breathing heavy."

"Mad little siren. And that bull part reminds me of Hemmingway."

"And I asked her if I could help her. She glared at me and lifted up her bike and broken painting and walked away, and as she did she said, "Jouez au diable" which means…"

"Go to the devil."

"And maybe you should've."

"Oh no, Bea. What that woman was, what she is? She is life to me. She is every breath I know. She is air and water and sunlight and now, she's gone."

"You make me wistful for my young life, Mont. Oh how long has it been since I felt that way about anyone or even anything for that matter, although I do have this Cartier tank watch. Well, I can't say what it is, but it just does something for me."

Mont started to sob deeply. His eyes were blind with tears. They rushed down his cheeks and dampened his collar.

"I held happiness in my hands. I had it right there." He looked down at his empty hands.

"I didn't know it. I did not know what I had. And now it's gone and I'll never find it again."

His head dropped into his arms. His shoulders shook as he wheezed and cried.

Bea looked around the room to see if anyone at the other tables was watching. Their waiter rushed over to the table. He looked at Bea in disgust and put his arms around Mont.

"Come with me, sir. It will be alright," he said in a fatherly tone.

Mont looked up. He dried his eyes with a handkerchief he pulled from his breast pocket and got up with the waiter. The waiter held him with his arm around his waist beneath his jacket and walked Mont to the front door and outside of the restaurant to the stairs where the stone jockey statues stood holding lanterns. They sat down on the brown stone steps and the waiter handed Mont a cigarette while taking one for himself.

"She was very special to you, this girl?" the waiter asked.

"How did you know?"

"You wear it; your heart break."

"Oh. You're very observant."

"Here have a smoke."

The waiter produced a pack of matches and lit the cigarette as Mont held it in his lips.

He lit himself one as well.

Mont inhaled deeply and then blew out a stream of smoke.

"Do you feel a bit better?"

"Remarkably, yes."

"Good."

"How did you get to be so smart?"

"I've worked here for years. We see many things."

Mont looked westward down Fifty-Second Street.

"I guess you've seen your share of heartbreak?"

"But also we see the joy."

"It's life isn't it?"

"It gets better, Mr. Clark."

"I hope it does."

He looked down at his black loafer. He kicked some dirt off the tip of his right shoe.

"And if she doesn't come back?"

"Yes?" The waiter inhaled.

"We have this expression at home," he exhaled.

"And?"

"Always there's another."

"But what about if there isn't another?"

The waiter took a drag off of his cigarette. He held the smoke in for a moment and then exhaled.

"Then you should be thankful for what you had and for the time you shared. Because that makes it precious, something you hold close to your heart. But, we must move on."

"That's the hardest part."

"Not so hard, sir. Life continues to gravitate. We start up in the heavens and end down in the soil. Anything that does not isn't alive. But even in death the body moves as it decays."

"And the rest of the earth feeds off of it as we become part of the over soul. Is that it?"

Mont took another puff as he looked to the waiter for an answer.

"I must go now."

"Thanks, Dominick."

The waiter smiled. He stood up and stepped quietly down the stairs, his back straight, he opened the doors and walked into the restaurant, with a linen napkin draped over his arm.

Mont could see Bea through the window as she collected her things and moved out of the restaurant. She closed her cell phone as she strolled out the entrance and over to Mont.

"I just called the driver. He's bringing the car around."

Mont smiled as he flicked his cigarette butt onto the street.

"Are you feeling any better?"

"Much."

She clutched her bag nervously.

"Is there somewhere that I can drop you?"

"Yes, perhaps over to the NYAC."

"That sounds like a very good idea."

"Right."

The limousine shimmied a bit as it pulled around the corner and up alongside the curb, nearly touching it. Bea held Mont's arm as they walked toward the car door and waited. The driver got out of the car and opened the passenger door. Bea let go of Mont's arm and stepped forward. She lowered herself into the car; the top of the feather on her hat bent a bit as she climbed in. Mont followed after her. The driver closed the door and forced a smile at Bea and Mont through the window. He quickly opened his door, slid into the front seat, started to whistle, but stopped himself, pushed the button to snap the locks closed.

"Driver, Columbus Circle," Bea said.

The driver muttered something inaudible and then put the car in to gear and spun away.

Chapter Three

The car pulled slowly up in front of the sports club. It's towers stretched into the Manhattan skyline. Mont found he was lost in a thought. The limousine door squeaked as the driver opened it.

"Give us a ring later then," Bea said.

"Sure thing."

Stepping out of the car his foot landed in a puddle near the curb and splattered water on to his sock. Grabbing his arm, the driver helped him to the curb and in a singular motion with his other arm, slammed the door shut, dashed around to the front of the limousine and climbed in. Within what seemed like seconds the limousine sped into the distance down Fifty-ninth Street. The doors of the clubhouse looked tall, heavy and foreboding as he stood there in front of the building contemplating and watched Bea's car vanish into the horizon. As the limousine moved away he could see his dear friend waving from the rear window. He smiled and waved back.

The massive raised paneled doors, centuries old, stood before him.

"Should I go in, or maybe get another drink somewhere else? Better go in."

Before he could think anymore about it he found himself climbing up the marble stairway. Opening the front door, a doorman peered out at him. Mont raised his chin and eyebrows, cleared his throat and proceeded into the lobby of the building. A concierge rushed up to him and handed him a silk, wrinkled rep tie.

"Is this really necessary?"

"Mr. Clark, you know the rules of the club. You can't enter without a jacket and tie."

"I have the jacket. Doesn't that count for something," Mont asked.

"Do we really have to have this conversation every time you come to the club? You know the rules. They've been in place for over one hundred years Mr. Clark. We won't change them today," the concierge lectured.

"At least not *to* day. But maybe **one** day. Did you know that they've relaxed the dress code at 21? I didn't need a tie there," Mont reasoned.

"21? You mean the restaurant," the concierge said as if the word restaurant were something vulgar.

Mont looked down, amused and laughed.

"Of course, Miguel," he said, smiling, "you're right. The 21 Club is a public place. And I don't want any old codgers, living or dead, getting their panties in a bind just because I entered the clubhouse *sans* tie."

"Very good, sir."

Mont grasped the tie and began to knot it around his neck. The concierge motioned for him to move into the coat checkroom.

"Oh really, are we *that* Victorian?"

Peering the servant looked down. A crashing noise broke up the silence as a self-important woman came inside, mumbling and carrying several bags and a yipping Chi Wawa.

Mont overheard the woman speaking.

"Has my husband called yet? Apparently he's gotten us accommodations here," she said rather disparagingly, " in one of your cramped, dank little rooms for one night until the Waldorf Towers are available. I must say that New York certainly is *not* like it was."

She threw Miguel the yipping dog, which he promptly passed on to a bellman, and one by one took her bags from the chauffeur and placed them onto the floor. Another bellman arrived and both boys escorted her to the elevators. Her complaints could still be heard as the elevator doors closed and the car ascended.

Mont adjusted his tie, fixing its dimple and bounced from the coatroom. Clearing his throat, he moved toward the stairwell a la James Bond. The door let out a loud creek as he bolted through and ran up the stairs two at a time. By the third landing he had to stop. Holding his knees he bent over to catch his breath. After awhile he continued up to the third floor entryway. As he walked down the hallway to the swimming pool he found himself humming the alma mater tune of Penn State and chuckling. A yelp and splashing came from inside the doors marked "Members Only Pool Area."

The doors stuck a bit as he pried them open. The tiled room smelled of ammonia and chlorine. He watched as a rubber-capped swimmer did laps up and down the length of the pool. The sound of the water splashing in the pool and against the sides seemed to calm him. The sound had a soothing effect. The water reflected squares of light on the ceiling and walls. Sunlight poured through the windows and skylight.

The swimmer slipped his goggles over his swim cap and looked up from the water.

"Mont, is that you?"

"Yes, Peter. C'est moi."

The well-toned athletic swimmer climbed up the ladder and out of the pool. Mont was a bit jealous of Peter's washboard stomach and chiseled limbs.

Peter was surprised to see Mont. His eyes scanned him up and down.

"What's with the tie? Have you transferred?"

"Oh," he grinned while fingering the tie between his fingers. "No, I wasn't wearing one and Miguel insisted."

"Now, Mont, you ought to know better than that. How long have we been coming here?"

"How long has there been a club?"

Removing his swim cap Peter wiped some chlorinated water from his tear ducts.

"Would you hand me that towel?"

He walked over to the side of the room. An attendant handed him a towel. He walked toward Peter and threw it at him.

"Do you have your togs?"

"I suppose there are some in my locker. But my head's a bit muddled and I don't really remember the combination."

"Never mind, I'll set you up with one of mine."

He patted Mont's ass as they walked side by side to the locker room, like teammates.

"Now it won't be a minute."

Sitting down on a bench in the locker room Mont remembered his days on the crew team at Huxley. His mind flushed with youthful recollections and invented victories. Smiling, he waited while relishing every second.

"Such bliss is this. This is what I needed," he thought to himself.

Peter returned with a bathing suit.

"Really? You want me to put this on?" Mont said as he examined the skimpy regulation Speedo.

"Come on, old boy. You're like my kin."

"Okay, but let the record show that there was some reserve."

"Duly noted, with reserve," Peter mimicked.

Mont removed his clothes and handed them to an attendant. He looked at the young man and said, "Please, extra starch in the collar and the cuffs."

"As you wish sir," the attendant replied.

Peter laughed. He noticed that Mont had developed a belly.

Sliding into the bathing suit, Mont felt as if he were trying to stuff salami.

"I thought we were the same size, old boy?"

"*Were* is the operative word. Damn you!"

They laughed.

Mont walked pushed through the locker room doors and out toward the pool.

"He can't breathe," Mont remarked.

"What does it matter, it's only you and I, just like old times."

Peter climbed the ladder, walked to the edge of the diving board, raised his hands into the air, took a deep breath, bounced twice, took a jump and did a perfect three-point dive into the pool.

"Show off!" Mont called after him. Peter bobbed to the surface.

"Come on, get in," he commanded.

"I don't think I can take it; the shock to the system."

"We're not that old, buddy. Come on. Swimming like drinking should never be done alone."

Mont examined the ladder as he walked up to the diving board. Upward with false trepidation, he climbed to the top and walked over to the edge of the board.

"You can do a belly flop if you like. I won't judge you." Peter said humorously.

Mont could hear Peter splashing around as he treaded water below.

"Okay," he called down to the pool. "But give me some room. I don't want to land on you."

He bounced a few times on the board. Everything about the spring in the board felt familiar and for a moment he felt as though he wasn't married wasn't a writer, and all that existed was the green sparkling water before him; he was just an adolescent kid on a summer holiday, out with his chum with zero worries.

The board sprang as Mont dived from it down in to the pool. The chlorinated air felt good as it brushed against his face and blew his hair backward. For a moment, on the way down, he felt as if he had been suspended in time, with the sunlight glaring through the skylights and the noisy filter buzzing and thumping out a rhythm like heartbeats. All at once he felt the water, first on his forehead and then climbing down his body like icy cold fingers enveloping him.

"A taste of death," he thought.

As if it were his second nature, he glided underwater easily, holding his breath and paddling his arms until he reached the wall of the pool marked 8'. Kicking, he zoomed to the surface and popped his head upward and into the air.

"Not bad, not bad a 'tall. You've good form. You haven't lost it. You'd make coach Brody proud!" Peter called over to him.

Mont shook his head.

"Ah, it feels good to disappear here," Mont said as he fingered some water from his ears.

"Should've brought my plugs."

"I'd forgotten how anal you could be."

"It's so nice to have a good swim."

"You know, you say that every time you come," Peter offered.

"Surely not every time?"

"Cheeky bastard," Peter cautioned, "do you want to race?"

"Really, I don't think I'm up to it," Mont said as he rubbed his arms.

"To the end!" Peter yelled raising his hand and index finger.

Mont started to speak, "To the end of…" and then took a quick dive in.

"Say, I wasn't ready that's…" Peter followed after him.

They sped down the pool but Peter easily reached the end hopped out of the pool and was sitting on the edge amused. He pretended to look at his watch when Mont finally caught up with him.

"I give up. You win. You are the victor."

Peter tapped the back of Mont's head.

Out of the pool Mont climbed up the ladder, clenching the rails as he huffed and puffed to regain his breath. Peter motioned to the attendant to bring over some chairs. The attendant slid some wooden chairs across the floor and then promptly brought two fresh towels to them, fluffing them as he walked. He placed them down on the chairs and vanished.

Peter handed a towel to his friend and took one for him. They laughed as they dried off their heads and bodies.

"You're getting fat, Montgomery."

"I'm married now. I don't have to stay thin, like you. I'm no longer in the game," he reasoned.

"Say, when you going to settle down?" Mont asked as he tapped Peter on the stomach.

"You know for a moment you sounded just like my Aunt Bedelia." Peter pat his face with the towel.

"How is old Aunt Bedelia these days," Mont asked.

Dropping the towel on the chair, Peter rolled his eyes and shook his head a little.

"She's got Alzheimer's, but we have her in the best of places. And she hasn't lost her sense of humor. Do you know the old gal gooses all the male attendants?"

"No kidding?"

Mont squeezed his rubber ass.

"I won't tell you what she did to me," he joked.

"And me!" Peter said, as he held his hand up to his mouth, feigning shock.

"But you're her nephew!"

"You don't understand English humor."

"I think I understand child abuse!" Mont said as he rolled his eyes.

"Dear old Aunt Bedelia. There's not an evil bone in that woman's body."

"And what a body!"

"I'm going to hit you hard, Bucko!"

As they walked into the locker room Pete put his arm around Mont's neck. "Let's shower quickly and get a bite to eat. I'm feeling a bit peckish."

"But I've just come from lunch."

"Tell me after the shower."

"Okay."

They each took a shower stall.

"Careful, you'll have to wait a bit for the hot water to get going. It takes awhile to come up through the rusty old pipes."

"I remember. But I'm no femme. I can handle the cold."

"Okay then."

Turning on the taps they shrieked simultaneously.

"Good gawd that's cold! I am a femme! I am a femme," he shrieked.

"I never knew water could get so frigid."

"Like your mother!"

"Like your father!"

"Oh mother of God!"

Mont covered his body in soap. His skin felt rigid, and bumpy as the arctic stream washed over him. Tension seemed to rise up his back and leave his body and he was all at once renewed. As he brushed his hands through his wet hair his mind seemed clear to him for the first time in weeks. The water temperature began rising slowly to warm.

"Figures... just as I've finished." He turned the knobs off.

"Isn't that always the case?" Peter replied. They dried themselves, shaking water onto the Italian mosaic tile floor.

An attendant walked over, took the towels from them and handed Peter his clothes.

"Have I been forgotten?" Mont said as he sat naked on the bench. Peter chuckled.

"Don't worry, Mont. I'll find out what happened to your traitor costume."

"Treading..." he cautioned.

Peter bounced and gave a chortle as he disappeared into the corridor banging lockers and whistling the Columbia University Alma Mater as he went.

Mont sat and counted the squares on the floor.

A few moments later his friend jostled into the room and threw Mont's clothes at him.

"Hurry up and get dressed. I want to get out of here."

Mont picked his clothes up from the floor and shook his head at Peter.

"What's there a fire?"

"You won't believe this, Buck. But I come here every day. It's like I'm still on the bloody crew."

He stepped into his BVDs and trousers. Flinching he buckled his belt. "Just burned four hundred calories. How many drinks do you think that is worth?"

"One if you're lucky."

"A bit stiff."

"You asked for extra starch in the shirt and they put it into the trousers."

"How'd you know?"

"Experience."

"Right, you said that."

"Yes, I find it's the only thing that centers me, relieves the stress."

Mont buttoned up his shirt.

"Your eyes are really red," Peter said, concerned.

"Don't worry, it's just the chlorine. It does that to them." Mont changed the subject.

"Is it really that bad working in the bullpen for your Uncles?"

Handing him the tie, he said, "You've no idea, it's like swimming in a tub of man-eating mermen."

Mont narrowed his eyes.

"Only you could come up with something like that. Mermen?"

"Well I didn't want to say piranhas or sharks, it's too common."

"I think we should leave the writing to me!"

"Right. So how is that going these days, old boy?"

A full Windsor knot found itself in his clutch. He adjusted the dimple.

"Could you get me a brush?" Mont called over to the attendant.

Feigning exhaustion, the attendant returned with a brush, comb and mirror. Mont brushed his hair as the attendant held the mirror and then handed the comb and brush back to the grinning servant.

"If you must know, it isn't, and what's that all about," he asked as he pointed to the waning attendant.

"Oh, he probably dipped your comb in the toilet or something like that."

"Great, I have literal toilet water on my noodle."

Peter patted him on the back and laughed.

"I've been meaning to read that little book you put out."

"You mean the one that won all those literary awards?"

"I've been busy."

"Swimming, obviously."

"I promise, Buck, I'll get to it before Christmas. I keep it right near the commode."

"You bastard!"

"I'm not kidding. It's the only place in the whole house where I can get any work done."

"Why? Who's keeping you up at night?"

He looked down. "I'll tell you about it some of these days."

"Okay."

Mont nearly fell as they dashed from the locker room like children and sprinted to the elevator. It seemed to take forever until the elevator car reached the ground level. They moved rather quickly across the lobby out through the revolving doors, the raised panel entry and down the concrete steps to the street. Some guests in the lobby scolded after them as the doors spun around. They caught every other word.

"Did the Baroness just call me an *incorrigible youth*?"

Peter rolled his eyes and smiled.

"I think she said, 'callow youth'." He straightened the back of his collar. "Just trying to bed you, dear lad."

Mont half smiled as he flicked Peter's ear.

"Fancy Essex?" Peter suggested as he rubbed his lobe referring to the Essex House Hotel.

"You know me, I could always use a drink."

"USE, is the operative word, Bucko." They hurried along the sidewalk of Central Park South.

"Nous sommes arrive," Mont cried as they entered through the Essex Hotel lobby.

"Oh, one thing," Peter said rather seriously, "if you're going to be seen with me, you can't be wearing the enemy's tie."

"I'd forgotten," he said, self-consciously, fingering the tie.

"Leave your 'ead at 'ome?" Peter answered as he tapped Mont on the crown.

Peter quickly undid Mont's tie. Peter held it in his hand while taking out a crisp fifty-dollar bill from his billfold and handed it with the tie to the coat check.

"Would you please see that this tie is returned to the sports club?"

"Yes sir," the coat check replied. She took the money and folded it into her pocket. As Mont and Peter headed toward the tavern, she threw the tie into a bin beneath the counter.

Peter and Mont took seats at a table across from the bar against the windows facing Central Park South. They had a nice view.

"There's no one in here," Mont said.

"It's early yet. They're still at work."

The bartender called over the bar to the boys.

"What'll you have?"

"I'll have a G & T with lime, and for my good friend Mont, a Scotch neat. And Barkeep, only the best please."

"Whatever you say, Mr. Halliwell."

Mont stared out the window at the traffic.

"There seem to be a lot of taxis out there today," he remarked.

"It's four o'clock, Mont."

"What's that mean? Oh right, tea time," he joked.

The bartender brought over their drinks and a bowl of nuts.

"No, that's when they change shifts, silly."

"Change what?"

"It's when the taxicab drivers change shifts. It's at this time that they have to refill the gas tank for the next driver. Look closely." He pointed out the window at passing taxicabs. "Do you see how none of the cab lights are lit up on either end?"

"Yes?"

"They aren't available for rides."

"But I know I've gotten taxicabs at four o'clock."

Peter wiped the sweat from the rim of his glass and took a sip.

"As if you've ever taken a cab in your life? Remember it's *me* you're speaking to."

44

"Right," Mont answered as he rolled a cocktail napkin up in his hand and held it closed.

"I'm going to have the man bring over some crab croquettes and cheese. It isn't Paris, but it'll do. Do you fancy anything?"

"I'm not hungry." He released the napkin from his grip.

"Oh that's right, you said you had lunch? Where? Who?"

"I was at 21 with Ms. Whittaker." He flattened out his collar self-consciously as he glanced out the window. His eyes focused on Peter.

Peter rolled his eyes.

"What's that all about?"

"You had luncheon with Bea?"

"So what's wrong with that? I've known her for ages."

"As long as I have?"

"Is that a rhetorical question?"

He held his glass up to his mouth, sniffed it for a moment and then placed it back down on the table.

"Mont, you've got to know that Bea is in love with you."

"What? That's absurd."

"She always had been."

"Since when?" He twisted the glass clockwise a few turns and then counter.

"Since we first met her. Don't be so daft and will you stop it with the glass?"

"Oh, sorry, nervous habit."

"In some ways you're still a boy."

"Right. And what did you mean by that last crack?"

"When did we meet Bea? It was some summer at the club in Westchester. We were playing doubles."

"Right, and Wendy," he filled his cheeks up with air and waved his hands out to his sides, "couldn't make it."

Peter laughed and nearly spit out his drink.

"So Bea stepped in," he said as he wiped his mouth with a napkin and regained his composure.

"So she did. She was a fair player. I'd say around a "B.""

"You're being funny." He wiped his nose.

"Oh, I just got it. Really, no pun intended."

"Mont, she was a "c" at best, but that's not what we're arguing. She took to you like flies to shit." He waved his hand in front of his nose.

"Must you be so graphic, Peter? It isn't in your nature."

"Swinging around with dead cats."

"What?"

"Never mind." He took a gulp of his drink.

"How long have I known you?"

"Since Huxley." He adjusted the cord to the blinds that hung in the window. Some dust fell onto his head and shoulders. He brushed off his jacket with his hand.

"Right. You had a thing for Maribel," he said as he placed the cord back into its holder.

"That old cow?" He smiled.

"You wanted to shag my nanny!"

Peter spit out his drink as he laughed. On his jacket sleeve he wiped his mouth.

"You have no idea how much this shirt cost me. And now it's ruined."

He brushed his eyebrow with his index finger and said, "Ask me if I care."

"I didn't get it off the rack like the thing you're wearing."

"It's only a shirt."

"Right. That's just your trouble, with you it's always only a shirt."

"Well you probably didn't pay for it either."

"I'll tell my tailor you said that. The truth is, we all pay, in one way or the other."

"Okay."

Mont took a sip of his Scotch. He picked up the lemon rind and twisted it over the drink and then dropped it into his glass and took another sip.

"So what's eating you?"

"I don't know that there's anything particularly *eating* me."

"Come now, Buck. I know you. This is bad. What is it?"

"She left me again."

"Petula?"

"Yes."

Peter took the plastic stirrer out of his drink and placed it onto the table. Mont picked it up and held it between his fingers bending it back and forth as he looked out the window at the passing traffic.

"How long has it been?"

"She's been gone about two weeks."

"What caused this new development?"

Mont picked up another cocktail napkin and crumpled it in his hand.

"Things haven't been good between us," he said as he stirred his Scotch and stared into its amber hue. Reflections of yellow taxicabs ran across the glass.

Peter called over to the bar, "I'll have the crab croquettes please."

He looked back at Mont.

"I'm sorry old friend."

"Bea seems to think that I'm better off."

"The bitch, she would."

"Ever since Pet got back from France," he paused, "she hasn't been the same."

46

"How so?"

"First her dog, Mrs. Hamilton, went missing."

Peter laughed.

"I'm sorry, I never got used to the name of the dog. Go on please. This is serious. I know. A bit of chlorine must've gotten into my brain," he tapped his brow, "apologies?"

"Accepted."

"So the dog is gone?"

"Yes. Mrs. Hamilton had gone missing. And then we were fighting *tous le temps.*"

"How long was she in France?"

"She went for about a month...goes every year."

"Did she visit with her sister?"

"She always sees Odette first. As you know, they are identical twins."

"At Clarenton?"

"Yes."

"When she came back home I was off doing a book tour. My agent had me traipsing all over the mid-west."

"So, you're a writer, that's what you do. It goes with the territory."

"No pun intended, I take it?"

"No, Buck. Go on."

"When I got back," he brushed a wayward bang from his forehead, "suddenly she wanted me to sleep out on the sofa." He rubbed his lip with his forefinger. "And then she was staying out late at night and coming home at noon the next day." His eyes caught the sight of an old woman as she pushed a shopping cart of bags along the sidewalk and then through the Central Park Wall. The woman disappeared into the park.

"She never did this before?"

Mont looked into his eyes. His brows furled.

"No, never before. We were always together."

"Maybe that's the trouble. I know what it's like to have you around 24/7. It can be taxing on the nerves. You are work, my boy.

"Not helping."

"So there's trouble in Camelot?"

"Petula said something about my suffocating her as an artist. She said that she didn't want to become what her mother was."

"This gets interesting."

"And then we went to an awards dinner at the clubhouse."

"That sounds fun."

"Right, I drag my beautiful wife into the morgue."

"Is that really fair? You did nothing wrong."

"When we got back to the house it started. She said that all the men and women at the club addressed me, but not her. She called me a *chauvinist.*"

"You may be many things, but that isn't one of them.

"And then she broke a few things, threw something out of the window, smashed the picture of my mother and father, grabbed her coat and slippers and stormed out the door."

"As she was leaving, did she say where she was going? Give you any hints?"

"She didn't tell me anything. She treated me like I was a roommate or something. She was very strange to me. Maybe she held me responsible for losing Mrs. Hamilton?"

"The French are funny about their dogs."

"I didn't mean to let the dog out. I guess I left the balcony door open. It was warm that day."

"And you have no air conditioner?"

"She doesn't believe in it."

"So you opened the door to the balcony off of the kitchenette and the poodle escaped?"

"But she never left the balcony before."

"No. That seems odd. But who knows? She was an old dog. Maybe she saw something running along Fifth Avenue and jumped?"

"I don't think her vision was that good. Besides, I asked the doorman and nobody found a body. If the dog were dead, wouldn't there be a corpse?"

"Okay, we have to find the dog and we have to find the wife."

"You make it sound so simple."

The sound of a clarinet and a piano drifted in from the back room.

"The musicians have started playing. Do you fancy sitting by the piano bar?"

He looked at Mont.

"I guess not."

Mont released the crumpled paper napkin from his hand.

"Bea said that Petula wasn't like us."

Peter smiled.

"You know, that's exactly what I like about Pet. She isn't like us Buck. She isn't like any of us. She isn't like anyone else I know on the planet. She's unique."

"What do you mean?"

"I know what Bea meant."

"What?"

"Hear me out before you interrupt."

"I don't."

"Buck, it has become your trademark."

"Go on then."

"What Bea means it that Petula Beaujolais isn't of our class."

"Upper?"

"Whatever."

48

The bartender brought over some crab croquettes. Peter took a slice of lemon and drizzled it on to the crab.

"But how does she know that when even I don't know that?"

"Quite frankly, it isn't that she knows anything. Bea is after you. She wants you."

"Me? Why should she want me?"

"Okay now listen to me. I've known you a long, long, time. You and me we go so far back I know you before you even knew you."

"I get it. Could you just get on with it?"

"What Bea wants is Mont proper. She wants the story."

"The story?"

"Yes chum. She wants that story-book life, the big house in Westchester, the fancy dress parties, the servants standing out in front of the mans when she comes home late from an evening at the opera. She wants the works."

"Oh come on. She isn't like that. I'm not like that. My parents aren't even like that. You know who's like that?"

"Who?"

"You, living like you're some kind of Royal."

"We will never be royals," Peter joked.

Do you have any idea how many times Bea's been married?"

"Exactly. She's been married five times. But her biggest score would be you, the handsome young novelist."

"I'm neither handsome nor young," he said as he dusted off his shoulders self-consciously and blushed.

"And the term novelist is questionable. One book does not a writer make."

"True."

Peter picked up a croquette and popped it into his mouth.

"The thing is, she wanted you. Sure she left you alone for a season or two while we were at Columbia. I think back then she fancied herself a fag-hag."

"A what?"

"You know, a woman that hangs around homosexual men."

"But we're not."

"This may surprise you, but a good many people thought that we might be."

"Why?'

"Oh, Buck, you are naïve. We did everything together. We slept together."

"We were sleeping."

"Right. We showered together. We had all of our meals together. We took courses with each other. I finish your sentences."

"At least you used to."

"I'm a little rusty but I think I could manage it."

"Yes, go on."

"And so Bea was happily content so long as she thought that we were a couple. And I don't want to kid you. She has cornered me a few times in the past and tried to drag the truth out of me."

"And so what did you tell her?"

"I was vague. I didn't give her an answer one way or another."

"And she fell for it."

"I was pretty good at acting."

"I know, I was surprised when you didn't pursue theatre as your major."

"You know that I wanted to."

"Yes."

"But it wasn't in the cards. Father wouldn't hear of it."

"So it's Finance."

"Let's not discuss it. It only makes me sad."

"Fair enough. Let's get back to making me sad, shall we?"

"So Bea left you alone. She was content riding in the back of our convertible while we went to the drive-in movie."

"You are funny. Maybe you should be the writer and I can muck around on Wall Street."

He popped another crab croquette into his mouth and followed it with a swallow of gin.

"I don't know how you mix the two."

He finished chewing.

"It's an acquired taste."

"So Bea thought that you and I were together, a gay couple?"

"Precisely."

"And it wasn't altruistic? You delighted in tormenting her?"

"You've no idea. I'd have gone to any lengths to protect you, Bucky."

"Maybe you *are* in love with me?"

"Like a boy with his turtle."

"And I'm the turtle?"

"Yes you are. You are a giant sea turtle, a big fat, clawing, gnarly, turtle. But I love that turtle."

"Gee thanks." He took a sip of his Scotch.

"So why a turtle of all things?"

Peter drank a sip of his drink. He poked at a piece of rind that was caught on his gum with his tongue and swallowed.

"Because weeks and weeks go by and we don't see you."

"Oh, I get it, like an amphibian who dives to the floor of the ocean."

"And only comes up occasionally."

"Right."

"I'd be lying if I said that I didn't miss this, the banter between us, our cozy raillery. And I'd have done anything to protect you and this."

"What?"

"What we have."

"I think it's called a *bromance*, brother."

"But unlike Bea, I was willing to let you go, if it made you happy."

"I think the gin is getting to you."

"No, hear me out."

"Okay, speak your piece. You love me. You miss me. Bea's a cougar. I get it."

"No I don't think that you do."

Peter grabbed the stirrer and put it back into his drink and stirred.

"Won't that compromise the drink?"

"Oh I wouldn't worry about it."

A couple walking outside the window began to quarrel. The woman slapped the man hard across the face and then disappeared into a taxi.

"See, she was able to get a cab," Mont remarked.

Peter smiled.

"Heroic driver rescues a damsel in distress," he replied.

"No doubt."

"But when you found Pet, or she found you, or however it happened, I stepped back."

Mont swallowed. His heart beat faster.

"Now keep calm, old man, Peter's here. I know that look."

He took a deep breath.

"Waiter, bring us some water."

A waiter came up to the table and put a glass down and then poured some water from a pitcher into the glass. Mont took a sip.

"Better now."

"Okay, better. It's just difficult for me when anyone talks about her."

Peter wiped his mouth with his napkin and pushed the plate of leftover croquettes to the side.

"I want you to do something for me before I go further."

"What is it?"

"Close your eyes."

"What?"

"Just do it. I want you to close your eyes and listen to me."

He closed his eyes. Peter took Mont's hand in his.

"Now repeat after me, Petula isn't gone."

"Pet isn't gone."

"And we will find her."

"And we'll find her."

"And everything is going to be just fine."

He opened his eyes.

"Do you really believe that?"

"I have the power to make it so."

Mont pulled his hand back.

"You do, Pete? Really?"

"Listen, good man. When you met that girl she stole away from me my very best friend in this life and probably the next. Do you think I'd let just anybody do that? Not bloody likely. But I saw how you are with her. She's like this beam of light, this laughter, and this intangible cloud. I understand. She's delicate. I never thought anyone could be like that. And her laugh it's like that of a little girl."

"And you don't think that I married below me?"

"On the contrary, I think she could've married better?"

"Better than me?"

"Yes, she could've had me."

Mont burst out laughing. He took a swig of his drink. "Just when I thought I'd heard it all." He continued laughing.

"What's so funny?"

"Nothing," he said as he held his lips shut and smiled.

"Okay, enough joking. There was a time when I thought possibly that you two couldn't ever make it. I mean you are like water and oil. They just don't mix. But you know what they say about opposites. And I thought, perhaps she is his split apart."

"How silver of you."

"But she has this other side."

"So you've seen it?"

"The entire campus has seen it."

"She can get pretty testy."

"Like a bull."

"I know, and I'm the bull fighter."

"No, I wouldn't call you that. You're more like the red cloth the fighter uses."

"Whatever. Can you get to the point? These Hemmingway references are killing me. I love that book, but please."

"She is a complicated girl. She didn't marry you for your money. She didn't marry a name. If she wanted your name she would've taken it when she married you. She's still Petula Beujolais."

"So what's your point?"

"My point is that Petula really loves Montgomery. She does. But she has to fight with everything you are."

"And what's that?"

"Your family, your history, twelve generations of Mayflower rubbish."

"But she said she was fine with it."

"She said that because she loves you."

"I never realized that it bothered her."

"No, of course not. You get so caught up in that writer's head of yours that you don't see what's going on out here, in the real world."

"When did this happen?"

"You've always been like this, since I met you at Huxley, from that first day, you with the old luggage."

"We met before then. You didn't want me to remember, and I've pretended to forget that little scene in grammar school."

"I was new to this country."

"What did we call you, *Peepot?*"

"Stop it or this drink is going in your face."

"It wouldn't really matter, I can always buy another shirt off the rack at Macy's."

They laughed.

"Besides Mont, Petula comes from a Royal family herself."

"She does?"

"De Rothschild, you idiot."

"I didn't know. She never said."

"Europeans are a little different about their heritage. They don't shove it in your faces the way Americans do. Titles here mean everything."

"Do you mean to tell me that she's titled?"

"Quite possibly."

"I never thought to look."

Peter sipped his drink. Mont muttered beneath his breath almost inaudibly, "Mother will be so proud."

Peter licked his upper lip.

"Did you hear yourself?"

"What?"

"I didn't think you heard yourself."

"Why, what did I say?"

"You said that your mother would be so proud."

"I did?"

Mont drank the last bit of drink from his glass. Peter looked over to the barman and motioned by twirling his finger, for another round.

"You mentioned your mother."

"I'm sorry."

"No need to be sorry, Buck. Every boy seeks the approval of his mother."

"And our fathers."

"I don't want to discuss him."

"I won't bring your Dad into this, Pete."

"We might have to."

"What do you mean?"

"Listen, have you filled out a Missing Person's Report?"

Mont twisted his empty glass on the table.

A waiter came over and took away the empty glass in his hand and picked up Peter's glass. He replaced them with full drinks.

Mont took a sip.

"You haven't, have you?"

"I didn't want to. I kept hoping she'd turn up. Bea says she's been looking for her."

"And you believed her? Please, Buck. The only place Bea has been looking is in the bridal section of Bergdorf's."

"*Vraiment?*"

"Yes, Buck."

"I guess I should get down to the police station?"

"I'd go with you, but I'm dead if I don't show up for work in the morning."

"No, I'm a big boy. I can handle it."

"And I'll see what I can do on my end. I'll talk to my father. We'll get Scotland Yard on it if we have to, and Interpol."

"I'll go tomorrow morning, first thing."

"You better, or I'll come up there to that cheesy flat of yours and whip you silly."

"Promises, promises."

He laughed.

"Let's finish our drinks. I won't even tell you what time my dear Uncles expect me in the morning."

"Business doesn't sleep. It's twenty-four hours, isn't it?"

"You've no idea."

Chapter Four

Mont showered, shaved and dressed, all very mechanically. He looked at the fog in his bathroom mirror. He wiped it and examined his face. His eyelids were heavy and he'd developed dark circles around his eyes. He tried to force a smile, as he had always done, every day of his life, but found he couldn't. He dug through the drawer of his armoire and found a grey hooded sweatshirt. He wore this when he felt the most vulnerable. He held it up to his nose and took a sniff. It smelled of her. She'd worn it last and then put it away – something he remembered having scolded her about. But now he was thankful. He wanted to get down on the floor and thank God that it hadn't been washed. These were pieces of her. "A section of my memory," he thought.

The stairwell down to the first floor felt narrow and dirty as he jumped two and three steps at a time. A splinter caught his palm as he slid his hands down. He moved faster and faster. On the landing between the second and fourth floors he took a tumble. A neighbor opened the door. An elderly woman in a pink shower cap looked out at him.

"Is everything okay?"

Mont picked himself up and brushed off his knees. "I'm fine. Just took a bit of a fall. I guess I was taking the stairs too fast."

"Well you shouldn't ought to do that. You could get hurt that way."

He extended his hand to her.

"Montgomery Clark," he said.

The woman held her robe closed. "Oh I know who you are."

"I'm flattered," he said as he smiled his boyish grin. "Do you mean to tell me that you've read some of my work?"

The woman scowled at him.

"No. What work?" She clenched at her robe. "I know you because I always hear you and your friends late at night climbing the stairs and making noise."

"You hear us?"

"I don't suppose you realize how loud you are."

"But we haven't done that in some time, Madame."

The woman looked at him with disdain.

"How rude of you. I am no longer married nor am I French!"

She slammed her door shut.

He rubbed the back of his head. "What the hell was that? I wonder who piddled in her Post Toasties?"

He continued down the last flight of stairs, through the narrow hallway and out the door to the street. He decided to walk the ten blocks down Fifth Avenue on the Central Park side and then over to the East side where the police precinct was located. The air felt damp. He found himself jogging and then stopping every so often to catch his breath and then continuing along with the walk and don't walk signs. Everyone around him seemed so apple pie ordinary. It was just another day in the middle of the week in New York City. He spotted the precinct from about a block off. He knew it by its big *globby masonry* – or at least that's what he coined it when his nanny had taken him by it in the carriage. His parents' original brownstone was not far from where he stood. He'd given up long ago walking past it to see who lived there, or if he might spot himself peering out from the past looking down upon him in the future from one of the upper floor windows-as he imagined he could do when he was a boy. These streets, Madison, Park, Lexington, had always held happy memories for him. When he walked through the old neighborhood of his youth happier times played tunes in his head and the scents and sounds of the upper eastside brought him joy, but not today. He was consumed with the task he held at hand. This was a serious business. It reminded him of all the things which one did not want to do, those uncomfortable, horrid chores that life requires of us. But he knew he must fill out a Missing Persons Form or MPR.

As he reached the police station his hands felt wet and clammy. He tugged on the handle of the door, as he did the door pushed forward and a Latin couple brushed passed him, smiling at each other. He made his way into the front room. There was a longish line of people. The front room was populated with police officers in uniform and men in grey suits and polyester clip-on ties. The room smelled of old cigars, dirt and soil from bygone and forgotten era. Some things in New York never change; they ruminate. The chalky smell of the waiting room reminded him of his boarding school days. His memories of sitting outside the Headmaster's office with Peter clouded his mind. He felt as if he could almost smile with the exception that he had this hollow feeling in the pit of his stomach and a pain at his side. "There's something very wrong with me," he thought, "there is definitely something physically wrong with me." Walking in to the room he took his place at the back of the line. He could hear different people as they spoke to the dispatcher at the desk, but their words congealed together into high and low pitched tones. He wallowed in his own tremendous sense of loss. After awhile it became his turn at the counter. The clerk looked up at him, "Sir, you waiting to catch a train or something? Step on up!"

He hurried forward.

"What's the story, morning glory?"

"What?"

"Why are you here?"

"I explained it all on the phone when I spoke with the officer."

"Do you have the officer's name?"

"I believe it was," he thought for a moment and fumbled with a receipt he had in his jacket pocket.

"Hedges."

"Officer Hedges?"

"Yes. I explained it all to him and he said I'd have to come down here and fill out a form."

"Right. Hold on a minute."

The clerk turned around and walked toward the back of the room. Mont could hear him yelling but couldn't quite make out what he was saying. Mont sensed his temperature rising. He watched the many different faces of people, - officers, and taking down reports at their desks, and victims, the expressions on the faces of the people in varying degrees of distress.

"She came out of her apartment and attacked me with her umbrella! She just bolted through the door and hit me. I did not provoke her. But she's lost it. It's dementia or something, Draza. And you have to do something about her. She's dangerous and a menace!"

"Mrs. Ogilvy is eighty-eight years old, Mr. Ignác. She's lived there all of her life. She says that you rang her doorbell."

"I did nothing of the kind," Mr. Ignác in his furry woolen chapeau, stated.

"Yes he did. He rang-a ma bell. He does this all the time. He's a dirty old man!" A woman in a floral kerchief blurted.

The detective looked up at Mont and smiled. She looked back at the couple. "Listen you two, either stop fighting or get married. You can't keep coming into our offices and disrupting us like this. We have serious crimes to attend to."

"You get that," Ignác said, "this she says is not serious. So then, *miláik*, what is serious? This woman says I harass her. This is not serious?"

"Please, Uncle Ignác. You and Irma have been going at it for twenty-five years."

"This from a girl you raised since birth? She talks to you like you are the stranger," Irma said.

"I promise I'll come and see you more often. I really don't think that the sergeant appreciates these dramatics."

"*Come* she says, Irma. She'll visit," Ignác replied sarcastically.

"After you are dead, then she'll come. You'll see. Like with Mr. Sherensky. Nobody sees him for days and weeks and months and then, after he is dead, Helena and all the family come, with goats even, from the old country. Then they visit when he is cold and silent."

"Please, Uncle Ignác. This is my place of work. We can talk about *this* later."

"A sheet over the head, that was all," Irma said as she motioned, "up the neck and down the side, with the cloth. He never got to say a final word."

"Listen, Draza, I will tell you what I can and cannot do. I am an American citizen and I can have the free speech if I like it."

"Okay. I promise I will come to your house on any Saturday that I am not working. We can have *veera*, and *raajky* at least once a month, but only if you promise that you will leave now."

"You wouldn't lie to your, Uncle Ignác? I'm an old man with a heart condition," he said as he held his chest.

"You aren't old," Draza said, smiling. She leaned over and straightened his shirt collar.

"From your lips to God's ears." He said as he brushed her hand away. "And I have a witness." He gave Irma's sleeve a tug. She looked over at him and grinned.

Irma put her hand up as if she were taking an oath.

"I heard it, Ignác."

"And you'll stop coming by with these phony complaints?"

"As God is a baker."

"I don't know if that counts."

"Sure it counted," Irma piped.

"Come, Irma, let's go. Perhaps we can find a bit of supper somewhere."

Mont laughed. Detective Draza Vucaru looked over at him.

"Is there something I can help you with," she asked trying to sound official.

"I've come to fill out a missing person's report."

"Was that you who called earlier? I recognize the voice."

"I spoke to Officer Hedges."

"He isn't in right now. He is out on a case. But I can help you."

She walked over to a desk and kicked at a file drawer.

"We've had these desks since about World War Two. They're made of airplane parts. You have to get rough with them in order to get them to behave."

She tapped at the desk and pounded on the top of it causing the lower file drawer to spring open.

"Eureka!"

Reaching in, she pulled out a crisp manila folder. On the tab was written very sloppily, **Mrs. Petula Beaujolais-Clark, Missing Person**. Draza pulled some forms from the folder and then deposited it back and slammed the drawer shut. "You can take these forms home with you and fill them out, or you can cop a squat over there and do it. It's faster if you complete them now."

"I'm all for expedience," he smiled. He noticed that her face had a sort of kindness about it and a glow despite her coarse manner and exterior.

"I am Detective Draza Vicaru," she said as she handed him a business card.

"Here is the MPR I need for you to fill out." She passed him a stack of papers.

"It seems like quite a bit of information to remember."

"Do you have any photos?"

59

Mont reached into his jacket pocket and pulled out his billfold. From it he produced a narrow strip. He handed it to Draza.

"Is this all you have?" She wrinkled her nose.

"Pet isn't very good about photographs. She likes to remember things the way that she remembers them, not the way that they actually happen. It's hard to explain."

"Where'd you get this from, some kind of carnival?"

"Coney Island. I squeezed her in to the photo booth all at once. I'd put the coins in. It was the only way I could get a snapshot of her."

"And there are no other photos?"

"I suppose I might be able to dig up a few more. And of course there's her student I.D. from Barnard. I'm sure that's still lying about somewhere."

"Okay sir. Take a seat over there and fill out what you can. You don't have to wait on line. When you are finished filling out what you can, come up to the counter and ask them to page me. I'll be in the back. Then we'll have a brief interview and we'll go from there. Okay?"

"Thank you. You have no idea—"

"It's okay. It's my job. Just fill out the forms," Draza interrupted.

"Yes."

Mont sat down on one of the hard grey metal chairs. He filled out as much information as he could. At times he wanted to cry. He thought that filling out the pages meant admitting that Pet was actually gone and that perhaps something terrible had happened to her – it made the loss seem concrete to him. He didn't want to think about it, but found he had to. "I have to get through these hard, uncomfortable things, these awful cheats of life. Damn you," he muttered to himself.

He held his stomach as he wrote. He read the line, clothing worn when last seen: note brand, style, patter, colors, & size for each.

"How the hell am I supposed to know what brand coat it was?" He scribbled: **Made in Paris**, onto the form.

After awhile he found his head had started to pound. He was having trouble with the descriptions. He didn't know everything item that Pet was carrying that night and didn't want to guess. He couldn't imagine what she might have carried in her pockets or her purse. He read the line, General Mental Health, Known Mental problems. He wanted to write something funny like *artist* but thought that they might get the wrong idea and not take the case seriously. By the time he reached the last page he realized that many of the slots on the form were blank.

"I guess I didn't know her at all."

He left the form on the chair and went outside. He pulled a packet of cigarettes from his pocket, popped one out and lit it. The street in front was packed with cars and trucks trapped at the light in a traffic jam. A man in a bakery truck honked his horn. The driver in the car in front of him called back, "where do you expect me to go? I have to wait for the light." Eventually the light changed and the traffic moved forward. Mont took one last drag and then flicked his butt to the curb and walked inside. A large Latin woman was sitting on the chair where he had left his MPR forms. In front of her she held a shopping cart filled with plastic bags that contained fruit, beans and rice. Each time someone tried to get out the door she had to move her cart so that they could slip by. A worker came by and said, "Miss, you aren't allowed to have that in here. If you are going to keep that here then you are going to have to put it out of the way. There's room over there in the corner for your cart."

"You mean put my cart over there where anyone can steal my groceries?"

"Miss you are in a Police station."

"Like that means anything. I bet more theft goes on in here than out there." She said.

The worker walked away, annoyed.

The woman looked at Mont. "Why are you staring at me? I had to come on my way back from the market. I can't make too many stops. I had to bring my cart."

"No it isn't that."

"You look pale. Come, have a seat next to me."

Mont looked down at the empty chair and smiled.

"Okay," he said.

"My name is Mrs. Miranda Gonzalez," she said as she extended a chubby hand to him, "so what brings you to this place?"

"I'd rather not talk about it."

"Oh. Drugs? Yeah, that's one monkey."

"No, Mrs. Gonzalez, it isn't that."

"Something worse?"

"My wife is missing."

"Oh. Then you and I share this same malady."

Mont looked at her face. She wore a heavy shade of blue eye shadow and too much rouge and lipstick. She looked to him like a poorly drawn version of a Brazilian Cabaret star, or drag queen. She smiled back at him. A gold tooth glinted and caught his eye.

"My Hector is also missing. He is my husband."

"How long has he been gone?"

"About six months."

"And are they helping you?"

"Miss. Vucari is very good. She's trying to find him."

"Do you know why he left?"

Miranda did not answer him. She reached into her grocery bag and pulled out a piece of fruit. "Would you like a pear," she asked.

"No, I'm not hungry."

"Fruit is good to eat when you're like this."

"Like what?"

"Empty."

"I don't feel empty, Mrs. Gonzalez. I am hollow inside." He thumbed his heart.

Miranda smirked at him, "Like you're the only one to feel this way." She snorted through her nose and then took a bite of the pear. A guard walked over.

"Now Mrs. Gonzalez, you know that you are not allowed to eat in here! How many times must I tell you? Every time you come in we have a problem."

"What, are we supposed to starve while we wait? You keep us in here for hours and expect us not to eat? Next you'll be telling me that I can't use the facilities. You are adding the insult to the injury, that's what this is."

"It isn't me, it's the rules."

"These rules are for the birds," she said as she stood up and grabbed her shopping cart and exited the station, while chomping on her pear. She dropped her pear into a bag and then scratched her behind as she pushed the door open and clanked her way outside.

Mont found the pages of his MPR crumpled on the seat where she had been sitting. He picked them up and attempted to flatten them straight. He looked at the doorway and grimaced.

"Could you please page Miss Vucari," he said to the clerk stationed behind the counter.

"No bother, I'm right here," she said as she came around from a corner of the office while munching on a sandwich. He handed her the forms. She licked her thumb, wrapped the sandwich up in some wax paper, grabbed the papers with her free hand and walked to the back of the room.

"Come on back here," she said as she wiped her mouth with a napkin and motioned him to sit at a seat next to her cluttered desk. She threw the balance of the sandwich and wax paper into a gray metal circular trash receptacle under her desk.

"Now where'd I put your information? I just had it a second ago."

She shuffled through papers on her desk. Mont wiped his forehead with his handkerchief. "Not helping," he thought.

"It's a little hot in here," he replied.

"I know the weather has been crazy. One minute we have autumn and the next it's like August. And in these buildings they never get the temperature right. It's like working in a sauna." She fanned a paper in front of her face.

"Listen, Hugo," she called out, "is it possible maybe to open up a window?" A voice from behind Mont grunted, "Yes, your majesty."

"We get so busy in here, I think after awhile nobody notices. Ah here it is," she said as she uncovered his forms on her messy desk.

"Just give me a second while I look through this." She popped in a piece of gum into her mouth, "interested?" she asked Mont, showing him the chewing gum package.

He shook his head, "no."

She chewed as she read the form and twisted a strand of her wavy hair around her finger.

"Very interesting." She said as she continued through to the last page. "This reads like a Romance or Mystery novel."

He smiled. "It's funny that you should say that."

She continued reading.

"You said something?"

"I'm a writer."

Draza placed the form on her desk.

"No kidding?"

"I wrote a book, a mystery."

"I'll have to look it up."

He looked at the forms sitting on her desk. Her eyes followed his. She chewed.

"So the way I come to understand it, you and your wife went to a party, came home and had a fight."

"Yes."

"And she left."

"Right."

"And you haven't been in touch with her since she left about two weeks ago?"

"No."

"What about your cell phones? Did you try to call her? Did she try to reach you?"

"We rarely turn them on."

"So you've had no contact with her whatsoever, and what do you mean that you don't use your cell?"

"These days the only calls I get are from my publisher. I'm falling behind in my work – missing deadlines, and they call me all day and night. So I just turned the phone off."

"So how is Mrs. Clark supposed to reach you if your phone is off?"

"My mother has the number for the landline."

"I wasn't talking about your mother. I was speaking about your wife."

"Oh? Petula? She has the landline number as well. I was confused, as she doesn't use my last name. She is an artist and is known as, Petula Beaujolais. It says so there on the form."

Draza read the form.

"Acrylics. Hmm. got it," she said as she continued to chew and slide her index finger across a line on the page. "So, if you don't mind my asking, what was the fight about?"

"She said that I was a chauvinist."

"And are you?"

"I don't think so."

"So why would she say this?"

"On account of the way the men at the club were treating us."

Draza wrote down some notes in the margin of the form.

"And this is a reason to leave you?"

"I suppose."

"Listen, were you having any money problems? That's usually the reason why couples split up."

Mont looked up at her. He wiped his upper lip.

"We had no financial hardships."

Draza pushed a bracelet up her wrist and twisted it. She put another stick of gum in her mouth and chewed.

"Oh I see," she said as she continued to read down the form.

"Trust fund?"

"Something like that."

Draza gathered up the pages and tapped them together and then put a paper clip on the top left corner. She opened the drawer, pulled out the manila folder and placed the forms inside.

"Is that it?"

"I think I have all of the information I need to go on."

He tapped the edge of the desk with his hand.

"So what happens now?"

Draza grabbed his wrist.

"I'll call you when I find out anything."

"You'll call me?"

"Yes. Turn on your phone. I need to be able to reach you within the next 12 hours."

"Will you know something?"

Draza got up from her chair. Mont followed, half-smiling.

"Let me walk you to the door."

She followed him. He opened the door for her, she passed by and walked outside of the station and out to the curb.

"Listen," she said as a tour bus brushed passed them on the street, she waited until the bus turned the corner, "my advice is to just sit on it for awhile. Nine times out of ten in cases like this, the wife comes back, unless of course there's another lover. But you mentioned in your report that you didn't think so. Give her some room and some space. If she really cares for you, and it seems like you think that she does, then she'll come back."

"And what happens in the meantime."

"In the meantime you grow up a little, answer your boss' calls and write that story. Believe me when I tell you that you should keep busy. Leave the detecting to the professionals and you just get busy with your work. If you dwell on it, you'll just go bizerk and that won't do anybody any good. Don't worry, I'll find her. I'm good at my job, graduated top of my class at the academy," she smiled, "now get!"

Mont laughed. He watched as she slipped back into the precinct and then walked with his hands in his pockets up the street to the subway station.

Draza returned to her desk grinning from ear to ear.

"Ah I know that look. I've seen it before."

"What are you talking about?" She said to her co-worker, Officer Lloyd.

"You've got a thing for the preppie."

"Nonsense. It's just the same old same old. I saw my Uncle today. I was just thinking about that."

"Then why'd you take on this case? You've got enough work already?"

"Who knows why any of us do the things that we do? I actually think I might be able to help him."

"Right," Lloyd said as he sat down and focused on his computer screen. Draza pulled out the case file on Petula and began to read.

Chapter Five

"Did you get the painting?" A thin figure in a long black cape and tight leggings said to the shadows as they came through the broken loft window.

"Yes we got it."

A young man, his mid-twenties pulled a hoodie from off of his head.

"What's with the bruise?"

"A bird attacked me once we jimmied the door open, Dette."

"In the kitchen there you might find something to combat an infection."

The man stood, stunned.

"Go then quickly before you drip blood all over the gallery floor. I've a show shortly and I don't need this!"

He scrambled through the dark room with its high ceilings and shadowy paintings hanging around. He wanted to ask her if she could turn on more light, but he was afraid.

She quickly removed the covering, which was tied around the painting to protect it during transport. She flipped it back and held the painting, which was about 3' by 3' square, toward the light. The heavily layered acrylic painting featured dancers and a Forrest and a gloomy bereft background of blues, grays, and darkness.

"So she did finally finish it.", Dette said to herself. "Finally, while all the time living with that monster."

The young man entered the room from the back as he rubbed his hands against his trousers to dry them off.

"That is the piece you wanted?"

"Yes, very good, Mike."

"And the payment?"

Odette rubbed the purple turban, which wrapped around her head tightly. She tapped her temple.

"And what was the payment to be, Michael?"

He cleared his throat.

"You said that you would give me eternal life."

"Oh, that."

"Yes, Ms. Beaujolais. You told me that you had the power to keep me young forever."

"And you believed me?"

"That you are a vampire?"

"Come here, my sweet," she said, smiling.

He waited a few moments. He was trembling. She motioned for him to come closer to her with her forefinger.

"Could we have more light please?" He asked.

"Are you scared?"

67

"A little." He chattered.

"I am a creature of the dark."

He could smell her. Her scent was of earth and soil, of blood, roses and forgotten promises. She pulled him closer and ran her long fingers against his biceps.

"You're a muscular little man, aren't you?" She said.

He smiled.

"It's not that I work out. I move a lot of paintings."

She kissed his forehead gently.

"What makes you think I can give you life?"

He pulled away from her.

"You told me you could."

"When?"

"That night in the village. You approached me. You knew me from the art world – you said. You told me that you were a witch, undead and that you could give me life. You said that you knew that I was going to die."

"I said all of that? I must've been drunk. I say these things when I am drunk. It was the vermouth talking, darling."

"You didn't seem drunk. And even if you were, you said you would change me."

"I've already changed you."

Michael stormed to the to the other side of the gallery. He stomped his feet.

"No need to behave like a child, Michael."

"But you promised. Do you even realize that I could've been arrested?"

He walked toward the back and flicked on the overhead lights. They lit up like stage beams and illuminated the walls of the room. The sides of the chamber were black and from the crown molding wires hung the extremely large paintings, which featured Da Vinci-esque garish figures.

Michael took a deep breath and calmed down. He looked up and marveled at the work.

"They look like…" he stopped himself.

Odette turned around and examined him. Michael stood about 5'7" tall with a flash of blonde hair. He was in his twenties but had a youthful air about him. His eyes were a piercing blue. She enjoyed his energy.

"Go ahead and say it, boy. Don't be afraid. I'm not going to hurt you."

"They look like demons."

"It's funny you should say that, I often thought the same thing."

"Are they yours?"

"I didn't inherit that talent," she whispered.

"What did you say?"

"No, they aren't mine. They were made by my sister."

Michael continued to amble around the rectangular room. The floors creaked as he tottered. It was cold.

"Can you turn on the heat?"

She glared at him.

"Fucking mortals," she said to the air.

She went to the rear and flipped a lever. Some heat belted down in waves from a vent in the ceiling. Michael stood beneath it and rubbed his arms.

"Ah, that feels good," he said as he took off his sweat jacket.

He wore a tight red tee shirt with the words, "Knitting Factory" on the back with sweat stains beneath his arm pits.

"What's that," she asked.

He smirked. "Oh that's from back in the days when I played in a band."

"And do you do that now? Are you a musician?"

"No. I'm also an artist. I paint as well."

She pressed her fingers against her lips.

"Of course you do, you little sprite," she flirted.

He grinned. Continuing to walk around the gallery, he remarked on the art.

"She's good, she's really very good – that sister of yours. I mean they are evil and scary looking. But also there's a kind of beauty in them."

"I'm glad that you think so. Let's hope the world feels the same way." She eyed the paintings.

"Do me a favor," she said to him. He walked back toward her.

"Yes?"

"Hand me my purse." She pointed to a pile of papers on a table near the wall.

He moved the papers, drawings, news clippings and sketches and found a satchel underneath it.

"Dig through it and see if you can find my cigarettes."

Michael felt around in the bag. His fingers felt wetness and stickiness. He pulled out a knife, which had a handle that looked like the foot of a goat. He placed it to the side on the table and kept fumbling until he found the pack. He pulled it out.

"If you aren't a witch, why do you have this?" He held up the knife.

"It belonged to my Mother," she said sweetly as she walked forward and picked it up. She held it in her hands and massaged the bone base. "Mother used it for cooking."

He looked at her and half smiled.

"Nobody uses a knife like that one for cooking. That's a ceremonial knife used in black magic. I may not be that smart, but I'm not that stupid. C'mon lady, give me some credit."

"You are cute. Do you really wish me to make you? You want to truly spend the rest of your existence with me?"

"I don't know. I don't think that I'd mind – if you'd stop pawing at me. At least my life would be longer."

"Why, are you dying?"

"I don't know. I think so."

"And what makes you think this?"

"A lover of mine died."

"Of AIDS?"

"His family said it was a heart attack." He glanced over to the windows at the moonlight.

"But I think that it was."

"And now you think you have it too?"

"I haven't been tested."

She snickered at him. He pulled back, still holding the cigarette pack in his hands.

"You don't honestly think that I give a damn, Mike, or what you think about my Sister's work do you?"

Michael looked down on the ground, crestfallen.

"I guess not. Pardon me for thinking that you had a heart."

He dabbed his eyes, which had begun to tear up.

She pulled the pack from his hands and sauntered over to the side, picked up her purse and tossed the knife inside. Popped out a single cigarette, she slid it into her mouth, drew a lighter from her pocket and lit the cigarette. She took another from the pack and lit that as well, clenching both cigarettes between her lips at the same time. She removed one and passed it to Michael. He waved his hand no.

"I quit smoking," he said.

"Why, why did you quit? This is madness. You're going to be immortal anyway, what's the point? This won't hurt you. Believe me, I know. I wish it would, but it doesn't damage. After a little while nothing will any longer."

"You make it sound like that's a bad thing."

"It is. After awhile you'll miss the hurt. The pain of loving and being loved will be gone. You'll miss the heartache disappointment and regret; the good and the bad."

"And the evil?"

She took a long drag off of her cigarette. She tapped her turban with her other hand and looked upward out the old factory windows which lined the top of the gallery near the ceiling.

"No, you won't miss the evil because it's always with us. We are the evil that lurks in the night. You wanted to know what she painted. That is what she had as subject matter. These paintings are in a way, all of me, of death, of disappearances. These paintings are of the things we can never get back, not ever; our fall from grace."

He looked to her pitiable, sort of mushed over in the corner. She moved to give him a hug, caught herself and pulled back.

"Weakness," she said to herself as she pressed her nails into her hand. Michael moved toward her and hugged her. As he held her shoulders, he felt the piercing cold of her bones – like nothing he'd ever felt before, it was like grabbing hold of a glacial lamppost in the dead of winter. He drew his hands off of her and looked into her eyes. They seemed vacant. There was something peculiar about them – like the light inside was omitted.

"What's a matter, kid?"

"Are my eyeballs going to turn like that?"

All of a sudden color rose up into her eyes, as if a toggle had been turned on and they seemed normal and hazel and then green.

"Like what?"

He shook his head.

"That was creepy."

She took another drag from her cigarette and handed the other lit cigarette to him. He took a long drag as well.

"Now how does that feel, Michael?"

She smiled.

"Good. Righteous. Reeeeeal good."

"You should listen to me when I talk to you. I distinguish things."

He took another drag.

"I never doubted you did, Countess."

He took another puff and looked at her.

"So all of this," he said as he waved the cigarette around motioning to the art, a trail of smoke following it's amber tip, "your sister created all of this?"

"Yes."

"So where is she now?"

Odette walked to the other side of the gallery. She adjusted her turban. She glanced down at the puddles of light the moon rays cast upon the gallery floor.

"I'm sorry. I didn't mean to stir the cauldron."

She turned around and faced him.

"No, it isn't you, Mike. It's just that," she paused. She flicked her cigarette to the side.

"I shouldn't have done that."

"Don't worry, I'll sweep up later."

"It's just that she died recently and I haven't quite come to terms with it yet."

"Yeah, death is a bitch."

He dropped his butt on the floor and stamped it out.

He looked up at her.

"I'm getting it, I'm getting it," he said as he picked it up and stuffed it into the pocket of his tight blue jeans. Some ash remained on his fingertips.

"Can I ask you something?"

She flashed him a flirty grin.

"I don't see why not."

"Why didn't you turn her? Why did you let death get her?"

Odette charged at Michael.

"You stupid boy!" she said as she lunged at him and grabbed ahold of his shirt, tearing it.

"Careful!" he cried.

"Don't you ever say that to me again. She was precious ma soeur. She wasn't like us, of filth and dirt and carnage."

"I didn't mean it," he said, pleading.

Her nails dug into him. They went deeper and deeper until blood trickled down through the rips of his shirt and on his chest.

She looked down at the blood and licked some of it off.

He watched her in horror.

"Your blood is sweet," she said as she continued to lap it up.

He held his head back. He enjoyed the feeling of her tongue on his chest and his nipples, gently biting.

She looked up at his face.

"You know, there is more than one way to become immortal," she said as she bit into his neck and drank. He moaned and cried and the lights suddenly went dark.

"Are you going to kill me?"

"I haven't decided. Being with you is like jesting with a half-dead mouse."

She felt his warm breath against her neck. He was breathing fast and she could feel his heart rapidly beating against her.

"Did you kill your sister?"

She paused and let him down.

"No. I did not kill her."

"Then how did she die?"

"She killed me."

Odette erupted in to tears. She bent over and hid her face in her cape. He forced himself up from the floor where he had collapsed. She sat on the floor holding her knees in her hands, sniveling.

He got down on his knees, weak from losing blood and crawled over to her.

"Hey, hey, it'll be alright," he said as he held his ripped shirt over his neck.

She gazed up at him and then buried her face in her knees.

"You say this to me after I nearly devoured you?"

He gazed up.

"You were going to devour me?"

"I don't know. Maybe. I hadn't had luncheon," she said matter-of-factly.

He moved a bit away from her.

"What do you mean she killed you?"

"When we were young. She was the pretty one, the bright star. And I was different. She always got all of the attention. No one ever paid attention to me. It was always about her. I was forgotten in the shadows."

"You're telling every artist's story."

She glared at him.

"Get me another cigarette."

He walked to the table and found the packet, pulled out another fag and lit one for himself and for her. He handed it to her.

She grabbed at it and quickly took a long hard puff.

"I spent a long time in perdition. But I knew that someday I'd get out. I thought that we'd work it out, you know, I'd come here and we'd be just sisters again."

"And so what happened?"

"She was feeble. It was too much for her."

"And?"

"And she perished in my arms."

"Just like that?"

"I watched as the life poured out of her."

He pushed some bangs off of his forehead, leaned over and kissed her on top of her turban.

"That had to be hard to take."

"Oh Michael, you've no idea."

"But you're here now and you have me. And I won't let anything harm you."

"Seriously," she questioned, in a stern voice.

"Not even sunlight." He smiled.

"Not even the light of day," she laughed.

"Say," he said as he pressed the top of her turban, maybe I'd need to stay mortal a bit longer, if only to protect you, my vampire friend."

She licked her lips with her tongue.

"Don't get any ideas," he whispered.

"Just cleaning up."

Michael stood up. He brushed off his jeans and walked over and foraged in the clutter until he found his sweat jacket. He put it on and zipped it up.

"I'm going to make some coffee. Do you want some?" He dabbed at his neck. "This wound healed pretty quickly, I guess you didn't bite me as deep as it felt."

She smiled.

"I'll have the coffee later," she said, "first I have to clean up this mess, or we'll never be ready for the show in time."

"You mean it about this 'we' business?"

"Yes," she said as she began removing clutter from the table, "I think having you around is turning out to be a very good thing indeed."

He walked over to the switch and just as he went to flip it, the lights went on.

"Witches." he thought to himself. "I'm a modern day Darren."

He made his way back to the kitchen, opened a cupboard and pulled out a container of Carte Noir. Carefully he poured some water into an ancient looking kettle. He rubbed his neck and wetted a napkin and dabbed at it as he waited for the kettle to whistle on the hot plate. He could hear her singing some French song in the gallery while she worked.

Once the kettle was whistling, he removed it from the plate careful to let it sit. He counted out for 30 seconds, "Because if the water's too hot it will burn the coffee," he mimicked her.

"I heard that. We can do without the commentary."

He carefully measured and ground the coffee in a tiny electronic grinder.

"Weighing the coffee is the most accurate method," he said, but as he grabbed the little cup, "but a scoop works just fine too."

He held it into the air.

Odette snuck up to the doorway of the kitchen and watched as he continued.

"It's important to grind your coffee right before you brew it whenever possible because a whole bean has much less surface area then ground coffee and it will help prevent those aromas and flavors from escaping."

She laughed. He was quoting her almost verbatim.

"You want to set to a coarse grind," she said as she came up from behind him and smacked him hard on his ass."

"Stop," he said, as he pushed her away. He continued,

"Now, we're going to pre-heat our beaker with just a little swish of hot water."

"Just a swish! I'll give you a swish!"

He turned on the hot water tap and waited for the water to steam. Once it did he held the glass shaft underneath."

"Would you get back in the gallery, you're making me nervous. I want to get this right."

"Just don't fuck it up," she said.

She turned around and he heard her as she moved back into the gallery space.

He dumped the coffee grounds into the beaker. He then filled it with the water just off the boil until about two inches below the rim of the beaker.

"The only trouble is she's Burr and I'm hopelessly blade."

He lit another cigarette and waited about four minutes as he watched the second hand of his Tag Heuer circle around. A crust began to form on top of the water. He gave it a stir so that all of the grounds interacted with the water. Then he carefully placed his plunger on top and waited. His four minutes were up. He began to plunge.

"Countess, it's done! Get in here," he called. She didn't answer.

"Come! You're always telling me that It's important to serve your coffee immediately because the coffee on top of the bed will continue to brew and become bitter and muddy. Either I brew just what you're going to drink or transfer it into a thermos! Which is it?"

He heard a loud crash from the other room. He ran outside. A painting had come crashing down and had fallen on top of her. He raced over. His heart beat quickly. There she lay, silent as a corpse, under the weight of the huge piece.

He tried to lift it, but it was too substantial.

"Are you alive?" he asked.

Her eyes fluttered.

"Don't move, I'll go and get help."

He shot up and nervously ran to the door. He couldn't remember how to open the huge interlocking bars, which held the gallery door shut.

"Where the hell are you going?"

He turned around. There stood Odette, upright. The painting was hanging securely on the wall, as if it had never fallen.

"But you were hurt. I was going to get some help."

"What, are you on crack?" She shook her head.

"At least I know if that did actually happen, that you are sincere, now where is my café au lait?"

He smiled.

"In the kitchen."

She followed him as he walked, "It's going to take awhile for me to get used to this."

She smacked him on the ass and laughed.

Chapter Six

The telephone rang several times before Mont heard it, as it vibrated against a broken glass on the floor. The back of Mont's head burned. He slowly opened his swollen eyes and caught a glimpse of the streetlight outside his apartment window. The phone stopped ringing. He rubbed the back of his head and felt a wet sticky substance. He opened his eyes and looked at his hand. It was full of blood. He picked up his cell phone instinctively and pushed a button and began to listen to his voicemail messages. A voice called over through the receiver, "Hello Mont, put the glass down and pick up the phone, it's Peter. Listen Buck; I have something to tell you. I think I know where she is; I mean I think we may have..." the message cut off. Mont dropped the cell on to the floor.

The landline started to ring loudly again. Mont rolled over and brushed some glass off of the receiver and picked it up.

"Hello Mont? Is that you?"

It was a friendly familiar voice.

"Bea?"

"What are you doing, darling, I've been trying to reach you all day?"

Mont sat up on the floor. He brushed some glass out of his hair and rubbed his eyes.

"The last thing I remember I was out at the club. I'd stopped by after meeting with the detective. I guess I had a few drinks too many."

He looked around the living room. Chairs and furniture had been turned on their sides. The French windows facing Fifth Avenue were wide open. The curtains blew in with the rain. He looked up and noticed that a painting Petula had done of some dancers was missing. All that stood in its place was an empty picture hanger and some twine. He also spotted a piece of brown paper that looked as if it had been torn from a paper bag, the kind you might find in a grocery store. It was taped to the wall.

"It must've been some kind of a night. Did the detective stir you up that much?"

"No Bea, it was just some of the boys from Huxley."

"Are you alright? You don't sound so good."

"Bea, I think I was hit on the back of the head. And it seems I may have been robbed."

"What?"

"The apartment, well at least the living room is topsy-turvy. And the back of my head is bleeding."

"Do you want me to come up there?"

"No, I'll be alright. It just feels like a bruise," he said as he rubbed his hand over the back of his head. "And one of Pet's paintings is missing."

"Now I know times are tough if someone stole one of those awful things."

"Careful, Bea."

"I just wanted to tell you to turn on the television."

"Why, Bea?"

"It seems there's been an accident. I think it might be someone we know."

"Oh?"

"Just turn on the television. Look, darling, I have to run. Unavoidable commitment ahead of me, the last one wants to come to terms. You know what that means, he doesn't want to give us the settlement we asked for."

"Okay, Bea. We'll catch up later."

"And do call the police, darling. I know it's a bother, but it's the only way the insurance company will cover your losses."

"I'm on it. Let me get to the television. Bye, love."

Mont hung up the phone, picked up the entire Bakelite, repositioned the round Victorian table that had fallen to its side, and sat it up and placed the telephone neatly on top, straightening out a circular lace doily. He shuffled through the furniture over to the television. He pushed the ON button. The dusty tubes took a few seconds to warm up. He hadn't used it in weeks. The news blared while images of the Hudson River and a helicopter flashed across the screen. A male voice blurted,

"Emergency crews in Westchester County launched search efforts for a missing man involved in a crash into the Hudson River.

A tow truck fished an Aston Martin from the Hudson River after a New York City man veered off U.S. Highway Route 9A. The blue two-door vehicle was seen inundated with water with two airbags deployed. Glass was on the pavement of the damaged roadway.

It happened in the Town of Mahopac just after midnight Friday. The driver, Peter Halliwell, 23, has not yet been found and is believed to have been swept away by the current. Emergency medical crews from Mahopac Fire and law enforcement from the Westchester Highway Patrol and U.S. Forest Service assisted in the incident.

Mahopac fire officials suspected no significant river contamination from the crash, according to assistant fire chief, Jim Brody, who was on the scene. Officials say the condition of the river and heavy rains in the area aren't making it any easier to find Halliwell.

The cause of the crash has not been determined at this time, but police are looking into whether weather conditions or alcohol possibly played a factor. The sheriff says that if the weather permits, they will continue their search Saturday for Mr. Halliwell."

Mont turned off the television.

"Oh God, Peter," he said.

He held his forehead. His eyes caught a note taped to the wall. He walked over to it and tore it from the plaster. The note read, "You killed my sister, now I will murder you."

Mont stared at the note as he held it in his hand. He tore some of the tape from the edge of it. The handwriting looked familiar.

"This looks like **my** handwriting," he said in horror.

He put the torn brown paper down on the kitchen table under a glass and fumbled in his pocket to find his wallet. "Where is it?" He pulled out some cards until he came to Draza Vicaru's card. He picked up his cell phone off the and quickly dialed her number.

"61st Precinct, Detective Arnold speaking."

"Hello, this is Montgomery Clark. May I please speak with, Detective Vicaru?"

"Hold on, she's in the break room, I'll get her."

Mont waited on hold. Self-consciously he began tucking in his bloodstained shirt and brushed back his hair. The pain in the back of his head seared as he brushed his hand over the bump.

"Hello, this is Detective Vicaru."

"Hello Detective, this is Montgomery Clark. I came in there yesterday to report a missing person."

Draza smiled. She picked up his folder from her desk and held it in her hand.

"You have to give me a little more time than this Mr. Clark."

"No. I have an emergency and I didn't know who else to call."

"Why, what's going on?"

"I was knocked out last night and it seems as though someone broke into my apartment."

"Don't move anything, I'll be right over."

Draza hung up the phone. She jotted down a few notes and then headed for the chief's office. He waved for her to come through the closed glass door.

Two uniformed officers passed her as she walked in to the room. She closed the door behind her.

"Still following leads on the drug bust in Canarsie Officer, Vicaru?"

"No, this is different. It's Montgomery Clark."

"The missing person case?"

"It's more than that, it seems that his apartment was broken into last night and he's been injured."

"Is it serious?"

"I don't know."

"And you want to follow up?"

"You remember what I discovered the other day." She looked out the window at the street. She watched as a group of boys played basketball in the playground across the street.

"Clarenton."

"Yes. It could be what we thought it was."

"Okay, but take Gonzalez with you."

"Thanks, Chief."

Draza walked to her desk and put Mont's folder into her briefcase. She walked to the back of the room where Gonzalez, a twenty-something Latino man was seated. "Chief says you're to come with me."

"Sound's pretty serious."

"It's 415, 417, and 242 possibly a 240."

"Huh?" He replied, nervously.

"Didn't they teach you anything at the academy? Chief is always giving me these newbies. I hope you know how to handle a gun."

"Very funny."

"Breaking and Entering, disturbance, assault and possibly assault with intent to murder." She smiled and tapped his police cap. "Don't worry, you'll pick it up after awhile."

"Thanks for the vote of confidence, Vicaru."

"That's Detective Vicaru to you."

"Right, officer."

They moved quickly to a squad car parked outside of the precinct. Gonzalez flashed the lights and siren as the sped up Madison Avenue to 73rd street. Once they'd pulled in front of Mont's building they got out of the squad car and approached the building.

"Do you think the culprit is still on the premises officer?"

"Doubtful. Mr. Clark said that it happened last night."

The officers entered the foyer and approached the doorman.

"We're here to see Mr. Clark."

"10th Floor, Apartment 10G." The doorman said.

They passed by an elderly woman and her dog en route to the elevator.

"I wonder what that's all about." She said. "I knew there'd be trouble if they let a writer move in here. See, Seymour, it's like I told you."

"Of course, Mrs. Finklestein."

Draza and Gonzalez entered the elevator. A boy in white gloves moved the mechanism and shut the doors. He took them to the tenth floor.

"I overheard Seymour." He smiled.

The doors opened to a small square room with two doors. Both doors read, 10G.

"Which door do we ring?" Gonzalez asked.

Draza laughed.

"This just means that he has either the whole floor or half the floor. One of these doors probably goes in to the kitchen and the other in to the parlor. My Uncle lives in an old building out in the boroughs. It's the same there. Let's try the door to the right. She walked briskly down the hall admiring the green, black and white mosaic tiled floor. Her heels clicked against the shiny floor. Gonzalez trailed behind her falling over himself. His gun kept hitting her in the back.

"Could you strap that holster tighter?"

"Sorry."

She twisted the doorbell until she heard the bell mechanism chime a few times inside. She heard a thud, a loud yell and then someone approaching the door. Gonzalez placed his right hand on his pistol.

The door slowly opened a crack. Mont peered through. He spotted Draza and smiled. He opened the door wide. "Were these scratch marks always on the doorknob?"

"I never noticed them before."

"Would you have an occasion to use a screwdriver or a knife to get inside?"

"Well not anymore. There's a trick to open the door." He said as he looked down at the knob.

"And you and your wife both know this method?"

"Well you kind of have to hold the door knob up a bit and then jiggle the door, insert the key and move it a bit this way and that," he motioned with his hand, "and then the door opens. It isn't hard once you learn the secret to it."

Draza turned to Gonzalez, "Snap some photos of this doorknob and then dust for prints."

"Yes Ma'am, but I have to go down to the car to get my kit."

Draza looked angrily at Gonzalez. "Just go!"

Gonzalez turned and made his way back to the elevator shook his head and then bolted through the door next to it and down some stairs.

"You'll have to excuse my partner, he's just out of the academy."

Mont smiled at Draza. She pushed passed him and into the apartment. Down a long hallway she hurried until she reached the living room. Garbage lay around the place, crumpled papers and ashtrays filled with cigarette butts. The coffee table in front of the sofa was piled high with dirty dishes and empty tin cans of soup, vegetables and Beefaroni. A pile of dirty laundry lay in the far corner.

"So I take it that housekeeping isn't one of your strong points."

"Pet always took care of everything. I'm sorry for the mess. Can I get you a drink or something?"

"No it isn't necessary."

"Do you mind if I have one?" he said as he went to reach for a bottle of Scotch from the mantle above the fireplace.

"I'd prefer you sober," she said sternly.

"Yes, of course." Mont retreated.

He rubbed his head. She pulled his head toward him and looked at the bruise. She brushed his hair back. It had already begun to scab. She pressed at the bump.

"Ouch."

"That's some bruise. And look at your forearm."

Mont looked down at his arm. There was a bleeding cut just above his wrist.

"Sit down, let me get you something for that."

"You'll find some handkerchiefs in the top drawer of my bureau in the bedroom."

Draza walked down the hall past crumpled papers on the floor and into the bedroom to her right. Blankets and sheets were piled on the bed. She had a little trouble opening the bureau drawer. She looked at the mirror above it and brushed her hair back. Across the room she noticed a vanity. It was very neatly arranged. The luxury makeup was neatly placed on a mirrored tray. Several bottles of perfume stood neatly in a line. It was the one clean corner of the room. As Draza opened the drawer she nearly gagged from the scent of death. She pulled at the handkerchiefs. A dead sparrow fell out of one. The front door squeaked as it opened and Gonzalez walked through. "Gonzalez, is that you?"

"Yes."

"Come in here for a moment."

He walked in through the door. "What the hell is that stench?"

Draza pulled some rubber gloves from her pocket and put them on. Gonzalez followed suit. "Here take this and bag it." She handed Gonzalez the dead bird. "I also want you to collect the broken glass from the living room floor."

She walked back into the living room where Mont was sitting in his armchair near the window. "Why are all her dresses on the floor?"

"We were going to a party."

"Is that the party three weeks ago?"

"The night she disappeared. I've been meaning to…" his voice trailed off.

Draza walked in to the bathroom and looked for some antiseptic. Every item in the cabinet was in French. Finally she spotted a bottle of L'iode. She grabbed it and hurried back into the living room. Mont looked at the empty nail on the wall where the painting had been hanging. Gonzalez crawled along the floor, gloved, picking up glass and chards with his tweezers and placed them into a bag marked, Evidence.

Draza took Mont's wrist and twisted it. She dabbed some iodine onto the handkerchief and then pressed the handkerchief against his cut.

"Oooowwwwww!!!!"

"Don't be such a baby."

"But that hurts. You might have given me fair warning."

"And then what?" She smiled as she applied pressure to his arm.

"Tell me, is there anything missing?"

Draza looked around the filthy room. "Would you notice?"

"Actually, yes. Pet had done an abstract post-impressionist piece of some ballet dancers. It was hanging there on the wall."

"Here hold this." She put Mont's hand on the handkerchief and stood up.

"Where over there, by that nail?"

"Yes, it was hanging there."

"There is some cellophane tape on the wall. Was something sticking there?"

Mont's head began to pound. He could feel the back part of his scull throbbing. "I think I'm going to need an aspirin."

"I'll get you one in a minute. Tell me what was here."

"It's there on the table. It's a note. But it looks like my handwriting."

Draza rushed over to the kitchen table. She found the note under a glass. A ring from the glass permeated the note.

"Nice way to damage evidence Mr. Clark." She shook her head and put the glass in the empty sink. She examined the note and then placed it into a plastic bag.

Officer Gonzalez got up with his bag and approached Draza.

"Listen Mr. Clark, we're going to have to fill out an official police report, but first I'm going to ask Officer Gonzalez here to run you over to the hospital to check out that bump on the back of your head. I also want to bring in a team to do a study of the place, see if we can dig anything up. Is the apartment exactly as you found it when you came to?"

"With the exception of the note." He looked around the room, "and the phone. A friend called."

"Which friend?"

"Bea called me. Bea Whittaker. Why?"

"We just need to know is all."

Mont went to stand and then fell back in to the chair.

" Come on, you take an arm and I'll take an arm."

Draza and Gonzalez walked Mont out of the door and to the elevator and down the stairs. She walked back and closed and latched shut the open living room windows. She stopped briefly in the kitchen and examined the lovely appointed china cabinet filled with delicately patterned china, Limoges, and tea service. "This is what the South of France must be like." She thought to herself. She turned off the kitchen light and the living room lamp, clicked her way down the hallway through the front door. She slammed the door behind her and caught Gonzalez and Mont as the elevator doors opened. The elevator boy looked a little shock as he spotted Mont's head.

"Mr. Clark has had an accident. We're taking him for some medical attention."

"Yes. As you say."

The doors opened. Once they'd gotten Mont safely seated in the back of the squad car, Draza radioed in code to the station. Officer Gonzalez dropped her off at the station and proceeded to take Mont to the emergency room.

Chapter Seven

"Darling, it's terrible," a middle-aged woman called to a room behind her.

Some newspapers shuffled and a chair scratched across the hard oak floorboards.

"Did you hear me, darling? I've terrible news."

She put some pink telephone pad notes down on the leather topped lamp table and turned toward the raised panel doors, which led into the library.

"Yes, I heard you. What's the trouble," he said. He pounded his chest a bit and let out a cough.

"We have some messages from Peter and then this morning…" her voice trailed off.

"Would you come in here? I hate calling across the hall. The servants will hear us."

"You and the damn help. Really Bill, you're such a snob."

He got up from his swivel chair behind his desk, smoothed out his trousers and stood up straight. Rubbing his lower back with his hand he shook his shoulders a bit.

"Well are you coming? I'll have Mary bring the breakfast out there."

"In the breakfast room?"

"Yes."

"But we almost never use that room for breakfast."

"Bill, you know that this is the year that I've decided to use all the rooms in the house that we never use."

"Right. I'd forgotten that."

"Now get up and have some breakfast."

"You know, Katherine, I have a very busy schedule today."

"Yes, dear, but you know what they say about breakfast."

Bill walked into the room. He tightened his belt as he walked. His loafers clicked across the parfait tiles in the hallway that ran horizontally across his path on to the Oriental rug across parlor floor way and into the breakfast room. He entered the breakfast room through a glass doorway. The windows faced the back garden and had a nice view of the Hudson River.

Bill carried his newspaper between his elbow and his ribs. He put the paper down on the table and reached in his pocket for his bi-focal eyeglasses. They weren't there.

"Gad, I left the darned things on the desk!"

Following, Katherine walked as if she were floating. Her hair was coiffed to perfection. She wore a simple silk, floral dress. Bill smiled.

"Really? Still?" he laughed.

"And after all of these years, you're such a boy."

"Married the best girl, didn't I?"

Picking up his paper she moved it to a table in the back of the room.

"Well I don't know about the best one, but certainly the most competent one."

"What's that supposed to mean?"

"Oh come, William Clark. You know exactly what I mean."

"She never even had a chance."

"That cookie cutter girl? I know all about her."

"I don't think you know everything."

"Yes I do."

He narrowed his eyes.

"Darling, you talk in your sleep," she said as she opened the paper and refolded it back to its original creases. Once she was satisfied she positioned it neatly against the wall.

"That was ages ago, and I'll thank you to give me back my paper."

"I will in a moment." Pulling his reading glasses from her pocket, she turned and handed them to him.

"Where would I ever be without you?"

"A darn sorry sort," She said in an Irish brogue. She laughed.

"You know, you did sound like Nana just then," he smiled.

Katherine looked up to the ceiling.

"And I am sure, William, that wherever she is, she still doesn't approve of you."

"Forgive me if I'm not mortally wounded." He joked as he patted his chest.

"Careful, darling, you'll hurt the crocodile."

Katherine walked over to the corner of the room and tugged on the rope twice.

"Are you sure it still works? I mean, we haven't been in here in ages."

"I had all of the chords checked last month."

"Really, darling you are a wonder. Wherever do you find the time?"

"Don't start with that, William."

Katherine sat down across from William.

A servant in a gray and white uniform with a neatly pressed apron came into the room carrying two glasses of water. She place one in front of Katherine and as she attempted to hand one to Mr. Clark he waved his hand, away. Katherine glared at William.

"Mary, better leave it. Apparently I'm not the boss in my own house," he joked.

"Mary put the glass down in front of Mr. Clark.
She left the room carrying the tray. Katherine got up and closed the glass door.

"Now I know that this is serious." He looked over at his wife.

"Is this about us?"

86

Katherine sat down. Her lip quivered. She started to cry. Clearing her throat, she grabbed a napkin off of the table, wiped her eyes and took a sip of water.

Bill looked over at her, concerned. He went to touch her shoulder but then pulled his hand back.

"I must say, I haven't seen you cry in a long time."

"I'm not a robot, Bill."

"Really, darling, let's have at it. I can handle it."

"It's not easy news."

"It rarely is. Let's have it."

"It's about, Peter."

"Who?" he coughed.

"Peter Halliwell."

"Sy's son?"

"Yes."

"I just played golf with him over at Briarcliff. He never mentioned anything."

"That's because it's just happened."

"What?"

"Apparently Peter was coming home, something about trying to help our son when his car…"

She stopped herself and took a sip of water.

"His car what?"

"He went off the cliff and into the river."

"Good God." Bill whispered under his breath. He took hold of Katherine's hand.

"I hate to ask the obvious, but is he okay?"

"They haven't found him yet."

Bill's eyes raced across the room.

"I see. Was he drinking? You know I've always said that these boys drink entirely too much."

"William, be charitable," she said as she pulled her hand away from his.

"Not to worry. I'll get some men on it."

"That's not what I meant."

"I should get them down there. You know, they won't look if they don't think it matters."

"But won't Simon handle it? He's in government."

"He's not in government, that's not government. Besides he's European and you know how that goes."

"So you tell me."

Katherine looked down and examined the floor. The tiles were shiny and she could almost make out her reflection. She rubbed the back of her hand.

The room fell silent for a moment. They were both lost in thought. Bill's eyes kept dotting back to the Hudson River.

"Pete's a good swimmer, crew, team and all that."

Katherine looked up. The doors clanked as the maid tried to balance the breakfast tray in her hands and turn the crystal knob to open the door.

Bill rose from his chair and walked over, twisted the knob and pulled the door open. Walking in Mary carefully placed two small juice glasses on the table, a pitcher of orange juice and a plate of whole-wheat toast with a container of butter. Carrying the empty tray at her side she quickly left the room, nervously closing the door behind her until she heard it click.

William scowled at the toast.

"Don't tell me this is your idea?"

"Not mine, darling, the doctor."

"I swear it's a conspiracy."

"William, don't swear," she said as she smiled. She handed him the plate of toast. Reluctantly, he took a piece, slathered it with butter and took a bite.

He looked up at her.

"Tastes just like butter," she said as she smiled warmly at him.

He smiled, chewed and swallowed the toast.

"No marmalade?"

"We've run out," she said as she delicately placed some butter on a bit of bread she tore from a piece.

"Now that I do not believe. Since when have we ever run out of anything?"

"You know me too well. I believe since Nixon, darling."

"That's President Nixon to you."

"Oh I don't know, I knew Dick, before you know."

"Of course you did, darling."

"Stay on point."

"So what else? I know you're holding something back."

He ate another bit, grimaced, held his napkin to his mouth and...she interrupted

"Don't you dare? I paid a fortune for those napkins and you are not going to destroy one just because you don't like to be healthy."

"Well how's about being happy?"

"You can be happy when I'm dead. Right now, you'll be healthy."

"And just what makes you think I'll out live you?"

She took another small piece of bread and popped it in her mouth. She smiled.

"The reason why I know you're going to outlive me is because I'm the one taking care of you. You are going to be the death of me William Harris Clark."

"And what a lovely one," he said, smiling.

"Look it's terrible news I have to break to you, but I don't think you'll think it so."

"Is it worse than poor, Peter?"

"Petula Beaujolais has left our Montgomery."

He tried to conceal his smile.

"William, try not to look so damn happy about it."

He poured a glass of orange juice from the pitcher into his glass and laughed.

"You know, Katherine, I've never made any secret of my feeling about the matter." He took a sip of juice. "I just never liked that tango dancer."

Katherine motioned and he pushed the pitcher toward her. She poured a glass for herself and cast him a disapproving glare. He looked up.

"It's not as if you always take orange juice. Sometimes you're on one of your crazy diets. I would've poured you a glass, dear, honestly!"

"That's not what the look was for."

"Then what?"

"Petula wasn't a tango dancer. That was Rhoda. Petula is an artist from Paris."

"I don't care who she was from what. She is terrible for my campaign. He knew this. He did this deliberately to upset us."

"Honestly, Bill, do you really believe that Mont is capable of that? You truly think he married her to spite us?"

"And that's another thing! Who gets married while they're at Columbia University, undergrad yet?" He cleared his throat. His heart started to race.

"Careful, darling, your blood pressure."

Bill took a pill from his pocket and another sip of water.

Mary entered the room carrying two eggcups with one-minute eggs on a smaller tray. She held her head down as she placed the dishes on the table. She looked to Katherine for approval. Katherine nodded. She left the room quickly. Walking over to the door, Katherine pressed it closed. William looked up at her. His brow creased into handlebars.

"When he decided to study English, I thought, fine, he'll got to Harvard, he'll get a law degree, he'll join the firm."

He tapped at the egg gently with his butter knife. She slid her egg away from her.

"Now he's trying at this writing business. What was that first novel about?"

"It was a mystery."

"Mystery my ass, Katherine! He totally dogged us in the piece. It was about you and I and what horrible parents we were!"

"What do you mean by that and don't be so vulgar?"

"He painted us as workaholics. The main character is a latch key child in a street gang. Any chance he gets he puts us down. Not to mention what they're saying at the club about us."

"Nobody is saying anything about us William, it's all in your head. If they say anything, it's that you're a bore!"

"Maybe I am a bit paranoid. But I am under a tremendous strain. I've got government at every turn, Katherine."

"Who asked you to? Do you honestly believe that my life is a bowl of cherries? It isn't like you ever consulted me before you decided to run for office."

"Let's not rehash that again."

"You didn't and I would've like to have been considered."

He dipped his spoon into his egg and scooped out some of the yolk. He deposited it into his mouth and swallowed.

"I do like a good one minute egg."

She glanced out the window at the grey sky and the rushing Hudson River.

"Yes, the new cook is really quite good."

"Sure is a shame about, Millie," he said as he dabbed at his mouth with his napkin.

"Let's don't quarrel, darling. I hate it."

She smiled warmly at him.

"I do love being married to you. You do know that, don't you?"

"Of course. Only you can put up with me."

"That cookie cutter girl never would've lasted."

"But when I think of the cookies!" He rolled his eyes.

"Katherine, there's no getting around it, Petula Beaujolais leaving is not a bad thing. The trouble is, Mont has too much money. He's had it too easy. Our parents saw to that."

"We never had so much."

"No, we did not. We had to work very hard, even when we didn't."

"I know it. But it's this younger generation."

"The "M" generation."

"I'm surprised you know that."

"I've had to become current and relevant for my constituency."

"So I see. Who is this new Mr. Clark?"

"Mont will be turning twenty-five next year. I won't be able to control his trust after that."

"So if she were after the money, she wouldn't have left."

"Perhaps, but we can't be too sure. Should I get some men on it?"

"I'm not sure. You're forgetting one thing."

"And what is that?"

"I think he honestly loves her."

Bill continued to eat his egg.

90

"A foolish folly on his part."

"Was I that?"

"What," he asked as he looked up at her. "Don't be silly. Our families knew each other for years. We were right for each other from the start."

Her eyes softened

A man in a dark black chauffer's uniform opened the door and entered the room.

"I believe I told you to knock first, Grantham."

"Yes ma'am," he replied. He adjusted his cap.

"Is it that time already?"

"Yes sir. We'd better hurry if you want to beat the traffic into Manhattan."

Bill got up. He kissed his wife on the head and pushed out his chair, got up and stood near Grantham.

"One thing's for sure, darling, I'm not doing a thing until Mont calls me. You know how he feels about being independent. That much I remember and actually it's one of the few qualities I admire in him. Even if he isn't independent, it's nice that he thinks that he is."

Katherine stood and straightened William's collar. He grinned.

"Don't work too hard at the office. And please be home on time for dinner."

"I'm not sure, I'll phone you later. Will you be needing the car today?"

"I've a million things – the charity ball for Phelps, and…"

"Right. Okay dear. Just send Grantham 'round to the train half past eight."

"That late?"

"It's a bear today."

"You could work from home?"

"We've been all over this. Presence in business is half the battle."

"I know, because accountability unchecked leads to…"

He finished her sentence, "corruption."

"I haven't forgotten everything they taught me at Miss Porter's."

"Wellesley, darling."

He hurried out the door. His valet met him at the front door and put his jacket on him and brushed the shoulders as he walked down to the black limousine. Grantham held the car door for him and he slid in. A geeky looking man in thick lenses spectacles was waiting inside with a half opened brief case and a series of papers.

"I'm certain it was Miss Porter's," Katherine said as she turned and realized he had gone. "And just like that, poof! He's gone."

Mary came into the room and began clearing the breakfast dishes into a tub.

"Tell me Mary," she said, "is there such a thing as a latch key wife?"

Mary looked up. "I'm sure I don't know, Mum."

Katherine rubbed the back of her neck, straightened her dress and left the room.

Chapter Eight

She could feel her palms sweating beneath her white gloves. She adjusted her hat and netted veil as she waited for the driver to open the limousine door. Grabbing hold of the chauffer's gloved hand, she stepped out of the limousine and adjusted the hemline of her skirt over her long, silky legs with her other hand. As Sergei, her driver helped her up, she raised her leg in the air like a Rocketed and stepped out on to the sidewalk – making an entrance, not that anyone was watching. Once she was standing straight, the driver hurried back into the car and pulled away. She watched as the limousine vanished in to the courthouse traffic.

"This is the last time I'll ever have to do this," she said to herself as she clutched her purse to her waist.

"Be brave, Bea."

She climbed the stairs and entered the courthouse. Flashing a pass to the guards, they helped her through the security monitors. She quickly found her way to the courtroom on the second level where she had been twice before.

"I wonder if he'll be there this time," she asked herself. "Of course he won't. He never has. But if he is, what will I say?"

She found a seat in a row about one third from the front of the enormous courtroom.

Pulling a paper from her purse, which contained some notes she had made, and some paperwork given to her from her attorney she began to read. Despite the fact that she had been divorced many times before, she found it a comfort to go over her "Divorce Crib Notes" as she had neatly scrawled across the top of the page. She read:

The hearing, if my lawyer is efficient, should only last about five minutes, isn't that what he said? But it may last as long as ten minutes? Can I bear ten minutes? My lawyer will tell me what time to appear. But was it ten, or eleven? I wrote it down. It's ten. I'm early. In Manhattan County there are usually not more than ten divorce cases on the court's call for final divorce hearings. What did he call them," her eyes circled around the courtroom ceiling. "Oh right, he referred to them as prove ups."

She looked around the room at a few other women and men who were waiting. She could feel the emotional tension in the room. She felt for her lighter and then realized that she couldn't smoke.

"My sequential place on the call depends on how early my lawyer asked for my case to be heard. But where is my lawyer? I don't see my lawyer."

She began to panic. And then she spotted him, a stout looking fellow in a poorly fitting Brooks Brother's suit.

"At $850.00 an hour you'd think Simpson would have clad him better."

She fumbled in her purse for some lipstick, held it in her hand and then let it fall back into the purse.

"I will sit here quietly in this gallery. My lawyer will be sitting towards the front of the courtroom at a table where lawyers sit. If I am not first on the call I will have an opportunity to listen and see the cases before me. I think this part will be interesting. When the judge calls the name of my case my lawyer, Sir Doofus," (she laughed), "will proceed to stand in front of the judge and I will make my way from the gallery to stand beside him. Because I am the plaintiff, my lawyer will tell the judge, very briefly, what the case is about. He will state the grounds for divorce and that there is a marital settlement agreement. After that the judge will swear me in. (I will take an oath or affirm to tell the truth.) My lawyer will then examine me."

She put the paper down for a moment. She looked over at a man in a pastel rose-colored suit. He caught her stare. He smiled at her. She smiled back.

"I bet I know what that one's about." She laughed. She continued to read, mouthing the words as she did, silently.

"The examination, consists of my lawyer having me testify as to what is written in the petition for dissolution of marriage, such as my name, address, occupation, Froggie's name, occupation (rich bastard), names and ages of the children (they're all his), grounds for divorce (I'm over forty years old), etc."

A tear caught her eye. She fumbled in her purse for a tissue and tabbed her eye at the corner and then pushed the tissue up her jacket sleeve. She continued,

"In addition my lawyer will have me testify as to the marital settlement agreement (MSA). My lawyer will show me the MSA and ask me if that is my signature on it. The lawyer will then summarize to the judge the provisions of the MSA. My lawyer will next turn to me and ask me if I understand the terms of the MSA. If, as is usual, there is a waiver of maintenance (alimony) then fatso will ask me if I understand what the waiver of maintenance means. The lawyer for my spouse may cross-examine me, but not if they know what's good for them!"

She flattened out a crease in her skirt and pulled it down over her crossed legs. She caught a man leering at her from the row across the aisle. She glared at him uncomfortably until he turned, embarrassed and faced forward.

"This cross-examination is not meant to put me on the spot. MUCH!" She continued, "the other lawyer will merely ask me a few questions to verify that I understand the terms of the agreement, and if there is a waiver of maintenance, that I understand the consequences of the waiver of maintenance. After the examination is finished my lawyer will hand the judge the divorce judgment the lawyer prepared and the judge will immediately sign it. I am then divorced again. The firm, before the prove up, sent me a letter spelling out exactly what will happen in court (which I am now holding in my hands, idiots!) and we set forth in writing all the questions which will be orally asked of me in court."

She put the paper back into her purse.

"But the big question we all want to know is, does Bea get the big prize? How much money will I get? That's the question that causes my stomach to do somersaults. Will the old bastard pay out? I need money to live. He's got to know that I need money to live. Haven't I always been good to the old Froggie?"

She thought back to her days when she first arrived in Manhattan, years ago, "by Greyhound bus, if you can believe it," she laughed to herself as she pulled at a loose string on her sleeve. "I'll never forget that first day when I moved in to the Evangeline on Gramercy Park, that boarding house for women. I was an model then." She smiled as she thought about the building and the way it cornered Irving Place and Gramercy Park South. "Even then I knew to choose a good neighborhood, despite the rules and the food. Oh, Bea, no regrets, remember?" She fingered a cross, which hung around her neck.

"Not ever," she said as she held the cross, leaned back and closed her eyes, hidden from the guards beneath her veil. She fell gently into sleep.

She woke abruptly as a female guard nudged her. The hat nearly fell from her head. She stood up and walked forward, straightening her cap, her stockings and her skirt as she walked.

Her case was the last to be heard by the judge. Her husband's attorneys did not contest a thing and agreed to give her exactly what she had asked for, 'out of love, admiration and respect, to free this wild bird' her husband had written.

It was an enormous sum, even for Bea. She had been angry at the time. This was to be her fifth divorce. So she had made the figure large, but her husband had doubled the amount she had asked for and it now equaled nearly half of his estate.

She felt that he was too anxious to be rid of her "and her hats," which had always been a bone of contention with him — since some of her hats cost the price of a small house in the suburbs, or so he had said. She felt that he'd have paid any number of the known money, to be rid of her.

"Oh, damn. He had to add in that last bit of poetry. Damn him! Now I'll have to go and feel sorry for the old bugger. Drats! Cats!"

Bea didn't feel free as she thought she would when she left the courthouse. She cried and felt sorry for herself, and him, and the life she had imagined she'd have had with him, if things had been different.

"I wanted this one to work," she thought.

It seemed like an eternity had passed her by since the time she first entered the court room and the final signing of the papers by the kindly judge who thought he knew her from a case before.

She walked out of the courtroom and in to the sun. It's rays beamed across her face.

"I am a very rich lady," she said to herself. "At least I'm richer than I ever was. And how much longer would the old codger have lived? But, damn! Damn! Damn! I wanted this one to work. I hate being single. It really says something about a person, and what it says, isn't very nice. Just imagine those girls at the Chanel counter now!"

Her throat felt sore.

"Where shall I go now," she said as she eyed her limousine out front. I know what I'll do." Smiling she skipped down the courthouse steps like a little girl. Sergei opened the door. Humming, she hopped in. He closed the door and they sped away uptown.

Chapter Nine

"Driver stop the car," Bea said as she reapplied her lipstick.

"I'm going to have to circle around the block. I can't just stop short like that!" Sergei exclaimed.

"It doesn't matter, Sergei. The entrance is on the side. Just pull up to the front so that I can get out."

"As you wish Ma'am."

Bea adjusted her hat and pushed back her hair.

"Not perfect," she said as she examined herself in the reflection of the glass that separated her from the driver in her limousine, "but it will have to do."

The driver had a little trouble opening the car door. The handle was jammed. He kicked the door. The vibration pressed against Bea's thigh, stinging her. Finally he pried the door open and she fell out and to the sidewalk. She looked up from the curb and waited. The driver extended his hand and helped her to stand. Bea brushed off her knees and skirt as she stood.

"Now I've got a run in my stockings."

"Sorry, Ma'am."

"Oh you will be when I call my service. Imagine them sending out a driver like you in a late model jalopy like this."

"It's a Lincoln, Mrs. Whitaker."

Bea felt sorry for her driver. He was trembling. She opened up her purse and handed Sergei a twenty-dollar bill.

"Listen Sergei, this is for you, not for your wife, or your kids. Why don't you go out and see a movie or something? I'll be in here awhile. And we'll forget the whole business about the door."

He stood, surprised.

"Don't look so bewildered, did it ever cross your mind that maybe I'm not as mean as everybody says I am?"

Sergei smiled. He tapped his hat and walked back over and in to the car. Bea straightened her jacket and walked up the granite stairs to the large steel carved front doors. A doorman inside pressed the door open and walked in.

"May I help you, Miss," a man seated behind a coat checkroom Dutch door asked.

"No, it's alright, I'll find my way in."

"I'm afraid I can't allow it."

"What?"

"This is a private club, Miss. Are you a member?"

Bea looked up at the chandelier that hung above her.

"Well honest to Betsy. You mean I can't go back there and find my friend?"

"If you tell me who he is, I'll have him paged to meet you here."

"Listen you little gutter-snipe," she said angrily. "It's been a long time since this was a Gentlemen's club. I can remember when Bella marched up and down in the front of this clubhouse to get them to let women into the membership."

"The ruination of the clubhouse," the man uttered.

"I heard that! And I take exception."

Bea began to roll up the sleeves of her jacket.

"Either you let me in, or I'm going to call some of my friends from the Ladies Guild and get them down here, and believe me, there will be more lipstick, perfume and estrogen than any of these boys can handle."

An elderly gentleman entered the foyer.

'What's the entire hubbub about, Fred?" he said to the doorman.

"It's this woman," the man said, as he motioned to Bea.

"Bea Whitaker, like a starlet from the heavens, he chimed."

"Oh Silas! I didn't recognize you. What ever happened to that goat thing you were wearing?"

Silas walked up to her and gave her a hug.

"Careful, darling or you'll crush the…"

"I know Bea, the gardenia." He pulled back and looked her up and down and said, "you are just as beautiful as I remember you."

Bea blushed.

"Well I don't really know what to say about you," she said as she rubbed her chin and laughed.

"Listen, how can I be of service to you? You know it's considered bad form to march in here an start threatening and belittling the help," he quipped, smiling at the coat check man.

"Silas, I spotted Montgomery from my car on Park Avenue and I thought I'd come in and see how he's doing."

Silas looked into the coatroom and stared at the 1940's light fixture. One of the bulbs had gone out. He stared back into Bea's eyes.

"I wish you would. He just sits there with his yellow legal pad. His publisher has called quite a few times, even sent a man down. We've tried to raise Montgomery's spirits, but you know how these writers are." He looked away as he pulled a cigar from his suit pocket and poked it toward the door.

"I have to have this now. My wife won't let me smoke at the apartment anymore. She says the dog has allergies."

Bea chuckled.

He nodded at the coat check man who wrote something in pencil down on a chart, as Bea walked past him, up the stairs and into the main parlor. She noticed a member's only sign with a silhouette of a man in a top hat painted on the side. As she walked through the large square room and high ceiling past several men who were reading newspapers, drinking brandy or cocktails, playing cards or talking, the room fell silent and each looked up. Her hat featured a large green Ostrich plume that fell sideways and poked a white haired man as she passed by. There were no other women in the room. She spotted Mont seated in a leather armchair near the window facing Park Avenue. He was writing something on his legal pad. He didn't notice her as she sat down in the brown leather chair that faced him. Between the chairs a round cocktail table crowded with three empty tumblers and napkins stood. She tapped the edge of the legal pad. Mont looked up.

"I hope you don't mind if I disturb you?"

A little disoriented, Mont rubbed his eyes until they focused.

"What's the matter, you look like you've seen a ghost?" she asked.

"It's not that, Bea," he narrowed his eyes.

"What is that on top of your head?"

"Oh this? Leftover from my Bonwit Teller days, darling!" She joked as she repositioned the hat.

"How'd you know where to find me?" He asked, looking at the other members who's eyes seemed fixed elsewhere.

Bea looked around the room. A few elderly men towards the back of the room eyed her cautiously and one winked.. She looked back at them and they averted their glances to the paper or card game or their conversations.

"Well if you must know, Mont, I spotted you from my car. We were going down Park Avenue and there you were. Since you aren't returning my phone calls I thought it best to see what's doing."

He smiled.

"It's refreshing to see you, Bea. You look wonderful, radiant. What's going on with you?"

She smirked and looked at the green flecks in his eyes. He looked thin and tired. He was unshaven and his blazer was wrinkled. The cuffs of his shirt were stained. His tie was on crooked and his hair was greasy. She could smell the hint of clove from his jacket. Pulling up the lapel of her blazer she sniffed her gardenia.

"I got the papers today. It's official!"

"And," he said boyishly, "Did you get what you want, the Chagall's and everything?"

"As a matter of fact, I did."

"And the money?" he whispered, looking around both ways like a kid caught in a scheme.

"Oh you are silly. In the end, Lazlo rolled over like a little dog." She tightened the bow on her fluffy blouse.

"That calls for a drink, don't you think?"

Mont motioned and a waiter came over.

"Till we stink!" He joked.

"Bring us some Champagne in a bucket, will you, my good man?"

The waiter nodded. In what seemed liked seconds he reappeared with an open bottle and promptly poured two hollow fluted champagne glasses.

"To my dear, un-flappable friend, Bea."

"And here's to you Bucky!" she said as they clinked their glasses together and took a sip. "Bottoms up! There's nothing like old friends."

"What is this?" She said, tasting something odd.

"Oh I'm sorry, it's Pet's favorite. I forgot." He bit his lip and quivered.

"Still?"

"Bea, you don't get it do you? Have you ever been in love? Do you know what this is like?" He didn't wait for her to answer but continued.

"I walk all around the city and I think I see her everywhere, her arm, her dancer's legs, that funny little wiggle she has. I see her hats and her hair blowing in the wind. She is everywhere. And then I rush to grab her and to hold her in my arms, but I find that it isn't her at all."

"I can't say that I've ever felt that way about Lazlo. He was a conductor. Funny, I thought it would be better with a musician. But it was worse."

"It seems like everything I say, or every other thing I say is something that she said. I hear her voice in my head."

"You could probably see a doctor for that."

"It's not a head problem," he put his hand on his chest, "the problem is in here."

Bea nodded. She looked out the window at the rush of passing taxicabs.

"And the things that used to bother me, like when she'd sit up late in that creaky bed she brought over from Paris with those stained knitted blankets and sheets from her grandmother's house, eating cheese and crackers well into the night, I used to hate her for it. She'd be on the phone with one of her friends or her sister talking for hours in French at the speed of light, so I couldn't understand her. And the crumbs from the crackers would litter the bed. I'd find them in my pajamas the next day. It'd be me and her and her dog, Mrs. Hamilton in that creaky bed, with her on the phone eating those silly little crackers and brie, and me trying to watch her pre-recorded French soaps or melodramas and thinking all the time that she was selfish. I felt like she didn't care that I had deadlines to meet or meetings or that I just plain needed my sleep in order to create."

Bea didn't know what to say about any of this. She thought about crumbs and bugs eating the crumbs. She opened her purse and dug around for a packet of mints.

"Those bed crumbs used to make me so angry. And her dog always seemed to be wet. How can a dog be sopping wet all the time?"

He reached over and poured another glass of champagne. Bea's glass sat full. He looked up at her.

"You're not drinking. Is something wrong?"

She laughed. She pulled up her blazer and sniffed at her gardenia.

"I was just thinking about the crumbs and the bugs."

He grinned. "There never were any roaches, Bea."

"Do you have to say that word?" She leaned over nudged his shoulder.

"You know they're in the walls listening to us."

"Now when I'm lying in bed and I don't smell the dog and I don't feel the crumbs or hear that horrible Euro music, I can't sleep. I miss it. I even miss the wet dog!"

He pulled a handkerchief from his jacket pocket and dabbed his eyes.

Bea tightened the bow on her blouse and looked down Park Avenue. She spotted a couple arm in arm.

She moved her chair closer to him and picked up his tie, slid the knot up and set it straight.

"You were in the hospital?"

"The robbery, you remember. I got a cut and a bump on the head. I felt fine, but Draza wanted me to get

checked out."

"Draza?" she asked, quizzically.

"I mean, Detective Vicaru."

"I see," she said as she played with some bracelets on her wrist.

"It was just a mild concussion. I'm fine."

"So you're good to go?"

"Go where?"

She took a sip of her champagne.

"You know, this is really is quite good. Pet has good taste, at least in champagne anyway, darling. But I have a proposition for you."

He sat up straight, smoothed out his pant legs and stared intently into her eyes. The blue of her irises played off the purple of the painting, which hung high on the wall behind her.

"I'm waiting…"

"Let's find spring."

"Huh?"

"Well I know it's somewhere this time of year, what is it, October? And Lazlo has graciously given me more dinero then I can spend in three lifetimes. So Mont, you've done so much for me…"

"That was only the once, and we agreed it would never happen again."

"Don't flatter yourself, you're not my type."

He laughed.

"Do you ever think Bea that part of your problem could be that you marry men twenty years older than yourself?"

"Listen, at my age and stage I'm lucky I get any action at all." The smile fell off her face. She was serious.

He spotted something in her eyes he hadn't ever seen before.

"Are you crying, Bea? I don't think I've ever seen you…"

"There's a first time, darling. Believe or not, I've actually a heart in there."

"You did care about the old codger, Laszlo, didn't you! "

"I don't know; Mont. Divorce is just *so* final."

"I know, I've been thinking about it too. I was thinking, what if she wants this? I honestly believe I'd give it to her, just as long as I knew she was happy and alive."

Bea reached over and he handed her his handkerchief. She dabbed her eyes.

"So what's the verdict? Will you come and find the spring with me?"

Mont's eyes circled as began to feel a buzz from the champagne. He spotted the waiter looking in his direction. He shook his head, no. The waiter returned to the kitchen.

"By plane, train, boat, or what?"

"I think that a little of each are in high order."

"So we're going red letter?"

"Does that mean you'll come?"

"I just have to wait for the publisher to cash my check. You see I've returned the advance on the new novel, had to. I couldn't get a word out."

He stood up and pulled Bea into him and gave her a hard kiss on the lips.

"Mont, what will they say?"

"Who cares, Bea? We're just friends, that's all, and they know it."

The men at the club applauded. Bea blushed and Mont took a bow.

"Travel will help, Mont. We will start by sea. I forget which titled Lady it was, a friend of Mountbatten or something, but she told me once, *travel by sea is best*. It helps to heal the heart. And let's face it, I think we both could use a heavy dose of that."

"I agree. Let's do it. You set it up and I'll send my apologies to the masses. We'll go Borneo in a big way."

Bea took a compact from her purse and examined her eyes. Some mascara had gooped up in the corners. She thought about getting up and going to find a Ladies' room, but abandoned the idea. She fumbled around for a pair of sunglasses. She found them and held them in her hand.

"I was thinking Ibiza. I want to have, Andres Monreal do a portrait of me or something," she said, motioning with her glasses.

"You cheeky girl."

"For the museum, Mont, don't be so vulgar!"

They laughed, and got up. The waiter approached him with a tray that contained his club card. Mont signed his number. He handed it back to the waiter as they walked out of the room. Bea's driver waited outside. Bea was so excited that she opened the car door herself, much to her driver's surprise, and got into the car and said, as she slid in, "I'll talk to you later. Now I have a million things to do. I'm so excited. There's shopping and packing and more chopping." She looked up, "do me a favor Mont, have your man send over your sizes. I'll do some shopping for you too!"

He giggled. "Whatever will make you happy!" He fumbled in his pocket for his cigarettes.

"You know something, I'm a little excited too. This is the best I've felt all month. Thanks."

"No you, thanks!" she said as she pulled the door shut.

Mont watched as the limousine pulled away and disappeared down a side street in the distance. The sun had begun to set over the skyscrapers of downtown.

Chapter Ten

As the water beat down upon her head rinsing the lavender soap from her hair, she felt strangely different. It was as if her body was not her body. She felt as though she were washing the body of a stranger. She continued down her silky skin with a loofah sponge. Over the crevices of her body, across her breasts and the lines of her last neck lift, along her scalp she traced with her fingers. She was removing dead skin. But the routine seemed odd today. There was something foreign going on. As she stretched her arms upward and followed with the sponge she felt her greatest fear. There was a lump under her left arm, near the armpit. It was distinct. She gasped. She didn't know whether it was from the steam of the hot water seeping into her mucous, tobacco filled lungs, or if she were just shocked by it.

"Now Bea, don't let's fall apart," she said to herself. "It could be nothing."

But she remembered how her Grams had died of cancer.

She turned off the knobs to the shower and reached beyond the shower curtain for a towel. Moving from the shower she dried herself off in front of the mirror. Rubbing some fog away from the glass she peered at her reflection examining the lump. It *was* there. She hadn't imagined it. She dotted the towel all over her body drying herself and then quickly put on her pink Lacoste Shirt dress and Tretorn sneakers. She tied a sweater around her neck, towel-dried her hair and tied it back into a ponytail, picking up the pink wall telephone she speed-dialed her chauffer.

"Ya?" a gravel voice answered.

"Sergei, I'll need a car at once. I'm going to see Pam."

Autumn was coming faster than anyone had anticipated. The leaves fell onto the limousine as it pulled up Riverside Drive and over in front of a shabby looking brownstone.

"I'll get out here and walk up to the building Sergei."

"As you wish Mum."

Bea nodded back at him. "Don't worry, Pam will sort this out."

"My wife and I will be praying for you, Miss."

"I shouldn't have told you. But if you can't trust your driver, well then…"

She opened the door herself and got out. The handle stuck a bit. She laughed and jiggled it. "It's not so bad once you know how," she said.

The door flung open and she got out. Once she was out of his sight line, Sergei fisted his face with his hands and cried.

Bea climbed up the crumbling staircase. She grabbed the metal rail, but it was loose and came out of its holders causing her to lose her balance and nearly tumble down the stairs. She regained her stance, took a deep breath and continued up the steep stairway. To her right on the landing there was an old metal bell box. There were several names. Finding the apartment buzzer that she was looking for she went to push but just as she was about to the door opened. A youngish woman holding a black cat stood at the door.

"Come in Mrs. Whittaker. Pam is expecting you."

Bea smiled, a bit alarmed.

"I don't know how she could be, I just came I didn't..." her voice trailed off as she noticed that the woman had proceeded to walk to the narrow staircase.

"Please shut the door behind you. Give it a good hard push and see that it latches shut. We've had some trouble with intruders. Take the staircase to the second level."

Bea turned around and slammed the door closed. When she turned around the woman and cat were gone, as if they had suddenly vanished. She shook her head and then walked up the old staircase, holding onto the banister as she climbed.

"You'll have to step lively." A voice called from above her. "I haven't got all day and I've squeezed you in as it is."

"Pam, is that you?"

"Of course, my child. Who else would it be?"

Bea hurried up the staircase. On the top floor stood a woman about five feet tall. Her hair was in pins neatly plastered against her head with Afro sheen cream. She smelled freshly bathed and of Witch Hazel. She wore large thick prescription eyeglasses. Her ankles were swollen and wrapped in ace bandages. She was holding in her hand a plastic shopping bag filled with yarn and two needles and in her other hand some knitting she had apparently been working on. Bea looked at the knit work as she reached the landing.

Pam caught her staring.

"Oh this, it's for one of the grandchildren. I knit them slippers every fall for the holiday."

"Christmas?"

"Kwanza."

"Oh, how nice."

"Get in here, child. You'll catch your death. There isn't much time and I've something cooking on the stove."

Hurrying to the door Pam guided her inside.

"Have a seat, dear," Pam said as she moved some old newspapers from what looked to be a sofa with a quilt draped over and covering it.

Bea sat down. The sofa was surprisingly comfortable. She took a deep breath as she sank into the cushion. The apartment smelled like baking. As she breathed in the scent she thought, "that's the smell of raisin cookies baking. She's making raisin cookies, just like my Grams."

Pam put her knitting down next to her side and took a seat in a swivel armchair. She watched Bea for a moment.

"Smell something good?" She smiled.

"Are you baking cookies?"

"No."

She looked away. There were pictures and what looked to be sacred articles all around the apartment. It was clean, but cluttered.

"Who was the girl downstairs, your granddaughter?"

"There was no girl."

"But I..." She realized there was no point in trying to figure these things out and so she decided to just move along with the matter at hand.

Before she could speak, Pam said, "I know all about the lump."

"How?"

"Your grandmother told me."

"Huh?"

"It's best not to try and decipher these things, my dear."

"Right," she said as she clutched her purse tightly in her lap.

"I want you to gaze into the ball. I think that's best. Let's see what's going on."

"Do you think...?"?

"Hush, child. Let the root worker do her work."

She felt uncomfortable. She shuffled a bit on the sofa. "And the cat?"

"There is no cat."

"Right," she answered under her breath, "of course not."

The old woman pulled out a step stool and began to reach up to a shelf above Bea's head.

"You'll have to forgive me, dear. But I haven't had to use it in some time. It's old magic, and hardly anybody goes by this."

She grunted a little and then let her arms fall to her sides.

"You're going to have to help me. My arthritis is acting up. I really should go some place warm for the winter. Each year I think I will get down to New Orleans, but there's always so much work to do here. Whoever said the city never sleeps, wasn't lying." She chuckled into her sleeve as she backed down the step stool. "But I don't think they meant it quite the way that I do."

She rubbed her chest and re-buttoned her cardigan that had been mis-buttoned.

Bea got up and helped her into her chair. She smiled.

"Now if you could just get up there, see if you can find a green box toward the back. It should be in there."

Bea took two steps up the stand and spotted the box. It was a little dusty. She pushed some dust off the shelf and reached in and pulled the box forward. She carried it carefully down the step stool. She was afraid she might drop it. By this time Pam had assembled a wooden folding tray table. She took the box from Bea and placed it on the table. She carefully removed the lid. The box was filled with cheesecloth and newspapers. She removed the

106

cloth and papers and took out a crystal ball. It looked dusty. She placed the box next to her near the bag of yarn and knitting and put the crystal ball into the center of the table. She placed an incense burner on a side table next and then asked Bea for a lighter. Before Bea could produce the lighter from her purse, the old woman held a match in her hand. It seemingly lit itself in front of Bea's eyes.

She swallowed hard.

"Now I want you to return to your seat."

She did as she was instructed. She put her purse to her side and sat straight on the sofa.

"Please take a deep breath. I want you to listen to your breathing. Breathe slowly through your nose and just listen to my voice."

Her heart was racing. She wanted answers. She had the urge to scram out of there. She had so many things to do and she didn't want to have to be doing this.

"There is no evil, dear about this that is necessary."

"But how did you know?"

Pam tittered.

"Close your eyes and take a few deep breaths. I want you to relax."

She closed her eyes. Her lashes felt sticky as she pressed them shut. "Too much," she thought.

"Take deep breaths. Breathe slowly. Let everything you are thinking about, clear from your mind. Empty your thoughts. Just listen to my voice and pay attention to your heartbeat, slowly."

She took a deep breath. Her heartbeat began to soften. She felt a calmness slip from the top of her head to the tips of her toes. She breathed in the smell of raisin cookies. She felt warm, safe, secure and loved. It felt to her as if a beam of light had covered her body completely, keeping her from danger.

"I'm going to count backwards now. When I reach the number one, you will open your eyes, you will feel refreshed and centered."

Bea tilted her head and arched her back. She felt good. She didn't want the feeling to end.

"Five, four, three, two, one."

Her eyes snapped open.

Pam had removed her glasses. She was cleaning the lenses with a cloth. She popped them back onto her head.

"Feel better now?"

"Much," she said as she fumbled with the knot in her sweater. She spotted a candle burning on a table near the window.

The woman cleared her throat.

"I want you to sit comfortably with your spine straight. This, child, will enable you to channel all the energy that comes through your body. This will ground you and help you to keep your mind calm."

Pam grabbed a cloth from her bag and gently wiped off the crystal ball. She threw the cloth back into the bag. She handed the ball to Bea.

I need you to hold the crystal ball and rub it with both of your hands. This will charge the ball.

Bea rubbed the crystal ball between her hands. As her palms moved across the sphere the ball appeared to become larger. She was beginning to lose her sense of herself and seemed only conscious of the detail in the crystal space, the larger the ball seemed to become. As she watched, she felt herself opening up, as if she had no edges or boundaries. She found herself losing her awareness of self and felt completely focused on the ball. Her eyes closed and she felt as if the crystal was all around her. She sensed that there was no difference between her and the crystal.

"I feel like I'm on ecstasy," she whispered.

"Hush, child and focus," Bea commanded.

"There are questions in your mind. Please ask them to the ball and be as specific as you can."

"What's going on with me," Bea cried.

Suddenly the room seemed to fill with smoke. Bea smelled something burning. The ball grew warm between her fingers. A wind rushed through the window causing the sacred items and brick a brack to clink against each other on the shelves. Pam clutched her seat cushion. Bea opened her eyes. The candles blew out. The ball grew hot.

"Don't let go of the ball," Pam said loudly.

The wind picked up around them blowing papers and bags and set Pam's blouse collar flapping.

"Stare into the sphere. Tell me what you see."

Her fingers dripped sweat over the ball. Her heart was beating rapidly. She thought she heard a jungle beat pounding out war rhythms. With all her might she turned her head against the wind, which had filled the room and looked into the ball. Her eyes were tearing and nearly blinding her.

"Fight it, just tell me what you see."

As she looked into the ball she saw a dark black cloud. She watched as it cleared and turned into a crimson colored mist, and then yellow and then black again. The ball cleared and then turned to silver. All at once she saw an eye. It looked familiar to her. And then she realized; it was Montgomery's eye. She dropped the ball onto the floor. It shattered and rolled toward the wall.

She looked up. The old woman was not in her chair. She looked down the hall and saw the old woman walking toward her carrying a broom and dustbin.

Pam huffed as she entered into the room. "I told you not to bring her here, Berta, I told you this would happen," she spoke into the air.

"Darned fools, bringing everybody who needs anything over to my house. Why don't your bring 'em to your house? Why do I have to always clean up everybody else's mess?" She swept the broken ball and glass shards into the pan, "That's not the point," she said, speaking to the air to an unseen entity as she dumped the waste into a burlap bag and then placed it under the shelf unit. I'm like a dealer cleaning up after a crack head. Done gone and wait fo' the high to be over, then out to the street so nobody see."

She looked at Bea. "Sorry dear, don't mean to complain, but this is a serious business we've got going on here."

Bea picked up her purse and clenched it. She looked into the reflection of the old lady's pupils.

"No you won't die. But only if you do exactly as I tell you." Pam placed the broom and pan against the wall.

"I will, whatever it is. Except crack, I won't do that."

"Silly, didn't mean to say that, Bea." She laughed, "damn white people." Pam opened her front door to the apartment.

"Listen carefully, you need to get in to that car downstairs and go directly to the airport. Then get on the next flight out of here. I want you to cross water – the ocean. Do you hear me, child?" she said sternly as if giving motherly advice to a wayward daughter.

"Pack?"

"You have to leave *now*. And do not take that boy with you."

"But…"

"We don't have time for questions. You need to leave immediately. You are in imminent danger."

"But…?"

"It has nothing to do with you, Bea Whittaker. You stepped into something. It has everything to do with him," she said as she helped Bea to her feet.

"And have the driver bring him here in a day or two." The old woman placed a business card with her name and number on it in to Bea's hand. "Have the boy call on me. But don't you speak to him. Not another ounce of your energy is to cross his. Do you understand me? I think I can hole up here for another day or two, if the spirits are willing," she said, looking up to the ceiling.

"Yes Ma'am."

"Now go, get on the plane and don't look back, don't you ever look back. Anything you have to do in the city, you can do from there. Take your trip, but leave the evil where it lies. I'll distract it to give you enough time so that you can get away."

Bea stood for a moment in the room, dazed.

"Go, girl! Now!" Pam pushed her shoulders gently.

Bea seized her purse and disappeared through the door. She wanted to think about what had just happened but found she had a sudden sense of urgency. Sergei waited outside with the car door open.

"JFK, darling, and step on it," she said as she hopped in.

"Somehow I knew you were going to say that."

Sergei slammed the door closed, got in to the driver side and took Bea directly to the airport in record time. The traffic seemed to part for them and every traffic light turned to green as Sergei approached it.

She quickly moved to the international counter and purchased a plane ticket for the next flight to Rome, First class and made it through the metal detectors just in time to board the flight.

As the plane reached 15,000 feet up and over the ocean she reached under her arm, almost instinctively, and pressed her fingers against her skin. The lump had disappeared. She smiled as the stewardess placed a chilled glass of champagne on the fold out tray.

Chapter Eleven

Sergei pressed hard on the buzzer repeatedly. Finally he heard a voice.

"What is it? Who's there? Bea, is that you?"

"No sir, it's Sergei, Mrs. Whittaker's man."

"Hold on, I'll be right down."

Mont shuffled around his apartment, dug through a pile of dirty clothing and pulled out a blue blazer. He popped it over his shirt and jeans, slipped on some boat shoes and dashed down the stairs and out the front door to where the driver was waiting, outside of the limousine with the door open.

Mont looked at him quizzically. "What's all this about?"

"Just get in the car, sir."

"Is it some kind of a surprise," he joked, "that Bea, always up to something." He got in and the driver closed the door.

Sergei drove the car down Fifth Avenue, across Central Park and over to Riverside Drive. He stopped in front of Pam's building. He reached through the window between the driver seat and the back chamber and handed Pam's card to Mont.

"And where do I go, in there," he pointed.

"Yes sir."

Mont got out of the car and stood for a minute examining the brownstone. Sergei pulled away.

Mont crossed the street and walked up the steps. Just as he was about to push the doorbell, the front door drifted open. He walked into the building. As he admired the mosaic-tiled floor, an elevator bell rang. Walking to the back of the corridor he discovered a tiny elevator, just big enough for two people, with high Victorian iron doors. A young man of about sixteen, (in uniform with a bell cap and white gloves) smiled at him while pressing open the elevator grate.

"May I help you, sir," he said.

Something about the boy seemed familiar to Mont.

"Sure, I'm going to the third floor."

Mont stared at the boy. He tried to place him. A monkey dropped from the open ceiling of the elevator car and landed on the boy's shoulder.

Mont looked over, somewhat alarmed.

"Is he yours?"

"Is anything ever," the boy mused, "he's a pet."

"And they let you bring him to work?"

The boy smiled eerily and didn't answer. The bell chimed and the boy moved the lever back and forth. When they reached the third floor, he moved the lever back and pressed open the grate and the double doors. Mont saluted, tapping his forehead, military style, smiled and walked past the boy

111

and into the corridor. When he turned around to say goodbye, the elevator doors were closed and the car was gone seemingly without a sound.

"That's strange," he thought. "But, Bea is always so careful about details! What a lark!"

The door to Pam's apartment opened. As she stepped out to the hall he walked toward her. She guided him into the apartment.

"Is Bea here? Bea?" he called.

"No, sir. She is not here?"

"I don't understand? What's all this about?"

"Sit down, won't you? I'll try to explain."

She took a throw pillow off of a chair and threw it on to a sofa.

Mont's eyes circled the room. He scanned details into his brain.

"I really like this chair. My grandfather had an armchair exactly like this one. And is that a pipe I smell? Tell me…what was your name again?"

"Pam."

"Tell me, Pam, does your husband smoke a pipe?"

A whistle blew from the next room.

"That'll be the tea. Please try to relax, I won't be but a moment."

Mont looked over to the window. The drapes were old and dusty and the sunlight seemed to barely filter through the sheers. He sat back in the chair and closed his eyes. "Borkum Riff tobacco," he thought. Memories of his grandfather walking him along the ocean as he collected shells flooded his memory. He could almost smell the seaside and hear the seagulls as they cawed against the backdrop of a gray winter sky. Pam returned carrying a silver tea service. She placed it onto a wooden tray table. Mont stood up and helped her to position the table between the sofa and his chair. Pam motioned for him to sit and she lowered herself down on to a divan.

"I see you've been looking around the room at my place. So what are your thoughts?"

"I have to tell you that I really do like the way you have the seashells lined across the fireplace mantle. My grandmother did the same at her house on Normandy Beach. She also had a collection of bottles filled with colored water."

"Will you pour out the tea?"

Mont removed an African print tea cozy from the teapot and poured out two cups of tea.

"Is there any cream or sugar," he asked.

"Silly boy. You don't take it with this kind of tea."

Mont picked up his cup, toasted Pam and took a sip. It was a berry tea.

Mont made a face.

"Bitter," she asked.

"Let's just say, I'm not used to it." He put the cup down on the saucer and slid it away from him.

Pam took a sip of her tea, then closed her eyes and smiled as she held it in her mouth for a moment and then swallowed.

"Nothing like a good cup of tea I always say. It's the warmth that does the most good. Tea has a curative power."

Mont began to feel uncomfortable. The air felt stuffy. He loosened his collar.

"I don't wish to rush you, Pam, but can you tell me why I am here? Is this some kind of a joke?"

Pam put her teacup down. Her face took on a serious air.

"I can assure you, Montgomery, that this is no joke."

Mont spotted some of the voodoo articles. He pointed at a statue of what looked to be St. Mary.

"It isn't who you think." She said.

"What is this place," he asked a bit angrily.

Pam stood up; she gently took the statuette into her hands and held it. She rubbed the face with her thumb.

"This is Isis."

"Ah, Greek Mythology."

"Yes, dear child."

Mont got up. He buttoned his blazer.

"Well this has been fun, but I have about a million things to do. You see I have this trip and…"

Pam put the figurine back onto the shelf and turned around.

"Sit down, Buck," she said sternly.

She took Mont by surprise. Only his closest friends knew his childhood nickname.

"I just want you to sit there calmly and listen to what I need to say to you."

"You sound so grave. What, did somebody die? And what are you anyway? Are you some kind of a fortuneteller? Soothsayer? Witch?"

Pam laughed.

"I am none of those things, and all of those things and more."

"She's talking in riddles," he muttered to himself.

"I'm not on any drugs, so you best get that thought out of your mind, and I'm not senile either."

"I'll tell you one thing, if you are a fake, you're one of the best I've seen."

"Have you seen? Really? Care your words, son."

Mont sat down.

"Okay, Pam, let's have at it. I've got things to do."

Pam looked up.

"You see, always the young in such a hurry. They rush to go nowhere in record time, and before you know it, their time has run out," she said as she looked up to the tin tray ceiling.

Mont felt as if he were in detention hall.

"Come, lad, no need to feel that way. This won't take long and then you'll be free to do as you wish, as always. I'm only here to help you."

"I wish somebody would," he said. "I only stay out of respect to Bea."

"I understand."

Pam produced a satchel of runes. She handed it to Mont.

"Please open the bag and pour the stones on to the table."

Mont did as he was instructed.

After he had poured the runes out on to the cloth he saw that there were five. Pam pulled the tray table closer to herself. She placed the teacups on the silver platter. A young woman in African dress came from the kitchen and removed the tray from the table and quietly disappeared down the corridor and through the doorway.

Mont stared at the runes and then up at Pam. Pam turned the table clockwise around an examined each rune as it stood.

"Tell me, what do you see," he asked, curiously.

"I'm a root worker, child, not a miracle worker. Patience please. I'm looking for what I don't see."

After a few moments Pam pushed the table from in front of her and clapped her hands into the air. The young woman returned from the kitchen. She placed the runes back into the satchel and put it into her apron pocket. She then folded up the table and carried it with her, vanishing into the kitchen.

"Okay, child. You may ask your questions now."

Mont cleared his throat. He took a deep breath and then looked into Pam's thick-lensed eyeglasses.

"You know what I want to ask. Why don't you give me the answers?"

"He came to warn you. I feel sorry for him." Pam wiped a tear from her eye. "He crossed over. If you want to know what love is, that is what it is."

Mont was confused. "What do you mean? Are you talking about Peter?"

Pam pulled a handkerchief from her blouse sleeve and wiped her nose. She stuffed it back into her sleeve.

"There are very few people who know about the sparrow."

He smiled.

"You were seven when you found him that morning on the window of your dormitory sill. He was hurt."

"I loved that little bird." Tears filled his eyes.

"Do you want to talk about it?"

"Do I have a choice? You know everything anyway, Pam, if that really is your name. Why don't you tell me? I like the way it sounds when the musical words come out of your mouth."

"It is no accident that you are a writer, boy. The universe needs to hear what you have to say There are truths that must be shared."

"Tell me about the bird. You said he crossed over?"

114

"You called him, Jerry."

Mont smiled.

"I'm sorry, it was a bit foggy – the reception is terrible in here today." She cleared her throat and continued,

"Jeremy, you called him, Jeremy."

"Silly name for a bird, I know it."

"You brought him back to health. You felt so alone there at boarding school. But he was your friend and you spent many days with him walking along the river and singing."

"I loved that birdie. He was my friend. But this is childish."

Pam walked over to the window and pushed the sheers apart, tugged the wooden bar of the block out shade until it flapped to the top and then opened the latch and the window.

"It's getting close in here."

"So tell me the rest. I want to get going."

"Okay, I'll try." She looked upward and shook her head at the painted over ceiling tiles.

"You put a dab of food coloring on Jeremy's forehead."

"I loved him. I wanted to remember him and it was paint."

"Yes, he came to see you the other day. He wanted to warn you. There are many people on this side and the next who love you and wish to protect you."

"You're going a bit too fast for me to process what you are saying."

"It has to be this way now. So just sit back and let me tell you what is going on so that you can do what it is that you must do."

"You're starting to creep me out, Miss Pamela."

"It isn't Pamela."

She sat down and rubbed at the ace bandages on her legs. "I'm getting too old for this."

"I'm sorry. I didn't mean to excite you."

"Dear child, I'm only here to aid you. Let me speak without interruption."

"As you wish," he said. He motioned with his hand for her to continue.

"First, your friend, Peter, his car went over the cliff. You didn't mention it. You didn't think about it. You've tried to block him from your mind."

"Is he dead?"

"It's hard to see, it's cloudy. This was the work of Boyce and Boice. They are an entity that work against mechanics."

"Will he be alright?"

"I don't know."

She smoothed the creases in her smock, took the handkerchief from her shirtsleeve and dabbed some sweat off of her forehead.

"Do you want me to get you some water," Mont asked, concerned.

"It isn't necessary, mortal," she replied.

She took off her eyeglasses and wiped the greasy lenses and then returned them to her face and let the kerchief slip into her lap.

"The harder matter at hand is your wife."

"Petula? Is she all right? She's not in any danger, is she?"

Pam tugged at her ear lobes and then scratched her nose.

"Always to find a way is difficult. To tell it so that you can understand, I find my words are failing."

"I can take it, Pam. Tell me what it is."

"Your wife is dying."

"What do you mean, dying? Is she sick? Where is she?" Mont's tone grew serious.

"Does the name Odette mean anything to you?"

Mont scratched his eyebrow. He looked out toward the open window. A loud radio blared from a car window as it passed by.

"Odette is Petula's twin sister. She is in an asylum in Paris, Clarenton. I'm not exactly sure of her illness, but I think Pet said it was Schizophrenia."

"It isn't."

"What does Odette have to do with this?"

"Everything and nothing."

"I don't understand. Can you be clearer? Pet just went to see her last spring. She's okay, isn't she?"

"One of the twins is no longer with us."

"Do you mean that she has died? Has Pet died?"

"No one ever does, truly."

Mont rubbed his hand across his lips. He could feel his pulse racing.

"This is frustrating me. You aren't giving me any answers. Where is my wife? Is she alive? I couldn't give a damn about her sister."

"That's truer than you know."

"Listen, Pam, just tell me so that I can go home and pack and leave."

"You aren't going anyplace."

"Okay, I think I've had about enough of your shenanigans. I'm leaving."

Mont stood up.

"Wait, don't go," Pam's head went down, as if she were in a trance. She began to speak in a familiar voice, one that Mont had thought he had heard before. His eyes focused on a crystal ball, which now sat in the center of the tea table. "Funny, I don't remember that being there before," he thought to himself.

Pam awoke, as if from a dream. She cleared her throat and played with some keys in her smock pocket and grinned. She looked at Mont and said,

"And the pink ones lose their pink-i-nocity forever."

Mont sat down. "I know who you are," he said, happily as if discovering the piece of a puzzle.

"So you know now why I'm here, don't you?"

"Those were happy times, Nanny."

"We made some good rhymes, child."

"But I thought you were…"

"Don't think about it. There isn't time."

"So tell me what it's all about. I'm listening now."

"This one, she's working magic, the Creole and voodoo kind. She is plotting a mean thing against you, boy. She is on a war path, out for blood and destruction."

"And where's my bird?"

"The werewolf took him. But have no worries, he isn't dead. He'll get free now that we've had our talk, and go back over."

"In the hollow of that tree where he lives?"

"Yes."

"Why would Pet want to hurt me? I love her. I'd gladly give my life for her."

"It's time for you to go now."

"But you haven't answered my questions and what was all that weird shit about?"

"You have all the answers, Montgomery. Now leave through that door and don't look back. Avoid the elevator and take the stairs."

"And so this is how you hand it to me? I thought you always hated loose ends."

"Nothing is as it appears to be. All I can tell you is that God did not take you this far, to abandon you. You are an agent for good. Always remember that. And we need more good in this world."

Mont felt a sense of release. He stood up, kissed Pam on the cheek and then walked out through an open door. He could still smell the scent of her witch hazel as he bolted down the dingy stairway corridor, through the first floor hallway, and out to the front stoop and to the street. He didn't know why, but he found himself running up Riverside Drive. He passed joggers, mothers with babies in prams and old men smoking cigarettes. It was a lovely autumn day. He sped across Cathedral Parkway until he reached Morningside Park. He stopped to catch his breath and looked across the street. He spotted a rakish blonde with spikey hair as she walked into Aesme's, a French café that featured coffee drinks, pastries and manicures. It was one of his wife's favorite hangouts. The blonde had a walk that seemed familiar.

"Maybe it's her hooker boots," he thought to himself. "All girls in boots have that step."

His head hurt. He pulled out his cell phone and pushed the speed dial for his car service. He gave the driver the address and then sat down on a park bench and waited. His mind felt fuzzy. He tried to process the afternoon. His phone bleeped. He had a voicemail from the detective. He wiped is eyes and waited. About fifteen minutes later his driver pulled up in a Lincoln town car. He stepped into the car, sat back into the seat, and felt relieved.

"That was some weird shit that witch doctor gave me," he thought as he dozed off. The driver turned on the fan and drove him across Central Park to Mont's apartment.

Chapter Twelve

She clutched her beige raincoat closed as she ran her house keys across the wrought iron gate.

"Listen, you've got to let me in. I have to ask my sister something."

The rain poured down and splashed in the streets, the sky grew dark.

She balanced her umbrella in one hand under her arm and attempted to tighten the knot of the scarf she had draped around her chin. Her skin tingled.

A yellow light flickered on in the window. After a few minutes she heard some noise. It was a door opening. A dumpy middle-aged woman in a nurse's uniform, stiff cap and black rain cape ran to the gate. She cursed in Creole as she fumbled for the key to open the lock.

"This night is not fit for man nor beast," she muttered.

Pet smiled, sheepishly.

"We haven't seen you in quite a long time, Chloe."

The nurse opened the gate and pulled Pet gently through.

"It hasn't been easy to get away."

"You're that busy?"

"There's a man."

The nurse smiled as she walked Pet up the stairs and into the building.

"Isn't there always," she replied.

An orderly peaked through a window in the steel front door and then unbolted the several locks and let the nurse and Pet into the building.

"Now you know the order. You'll have to sign in first, no exceptions. We didn't like that last bit of business you tried."

"But she's my sister and I couldn't wait."

"Right, you're so busy with your schedule. We have schedules here too. And we like to have her ready for your visits."

"But I don't like her like that. I don't like her with the drugs. She's dopey. She doesn't talk right and I need to ask her things. I'm her twin."

"You're talking to me like I don't know about these things. Listen dear, I understand. But you are no different than any of the other families. We have to show respect for everyone here. I have a heart, which is why I let you in at all, and after visiting hours."

"I do appreciate it." She smiled.

"Well it's nice to see you smile," she said, sounding almost motherly.

"So thin, whatever she's doing, it isn't working for her," the nurse thought.

"Can I get you a cup of café au lait, or some of those nice chocolate biscuits you like so much?"

"You are too kind. Thank you. I'd like that. I haven't had a bite to eat since I left the airport."

"Come over here dear and have a nice sit, and I'll be back before you can say, Girard D'Estang."

The nurse left the waiting foyer and hurried through a series of doors. Pet could hear them as the nurse jiggled the keys, opened the locks, and slammed the doors shut behind her, door after door after door.

She shivered a bit as she sat in her seat. She clutched her wet raincoat closed.

* * *

"I thought you'd come."

Pet smelled the distinct odor of floral, flowers, bouquets, and sunshine…yes, if sunshine had a scent – this would be it. She opened her eyes.

The sun glared through the windows. She saw a form but couldn't make it out. The light blinded her.

"Who is there?"

"Surely you remember me, Odette?"

"Odette, is that you?"

"Yes, my sweet."

"But how did you get out?"

Odette, a thin girl in a gray uniform and pink cardigan sat next to Pet.

"Listen darling, they're about ready to let me out anyway. I've been so good."

Pet smiled. She brushed her hand against Odette's cheek.

"You look worried. Don't be. I'm fine, really I am. I don't think I've ever been so fine."

"But why wasn't I informed? If they are to let you out wouldn't someone have notified me?"

Odette got up.

"Say, have you a cigarette?"

Pet fumbled through her jacket pocket. She pulled out a crumpled packet.

"But they don't…"

Before she could finish her sentence Odette had the fag in her mouth. She pulled some matches from her uniform pocket and lit the smoke. She inhaled deeply and closed her eyes. She smiled and held the smoke in her lungs for about thirty seconds. Then she blew it out in smoke rings and gave a wide grin.

"I'll tell you Pet, it's just like they say. When you haven't had a good smoke in a long time, it's like paradise, it really is," she rolled her eyes, "well if I knew what paradise was."

Pet looked nervously at the corridor.

"But won't old Mrs. whatever her name is have something to say about it?"

"The trouble with you Pet is that you worry too much."

121

"Worry? I don't worry."

Odette took in another drag and looked out the window. She held her hand to her elbow and fidgeted a bit with the cigarette, flicking ashes onto the freshly polished marble floor.   She spoke as she looked out the heavily barred windows.

"It's him again isn't it, Pet?"

Pet looked down on the floor. She took her foot and slid it over the flicked ashes until they disappeared.

"Look, I'll blow the smoke into the vent here," she pointed to a heating vent under the window, if you're worried."

She exhaled into the vent and the smoke filtered outside.

Odette smiled. "They're broken. They work the wrong way. Instead of forcing the heat out, they're sucking it in. We've a joke about it, we girls in the back, but I won't bore you with it now."

Pet looked up.

"Oh, I am sorry, Odette. It's just been a very long day and an even longer trip."

"You don't look quite your cheery, usual self."

"I'm not." She rubbed her forehead.

"When was the last time I saw you?"

"I don't remember."

She took another drag of her cigarette. She tapped the tip over her index finger.

"You were wearing that yellow frock."

Pet grinned.

"Oh I remember. It was the canary yellow dress. Oh yes, it was Easter, Odette. I came to see you on Easter."

"Right."

Odette flicked the cigarette to the floor and stomped it out.

Pet took a tissue from her pocket and picked it up and slid it into her pocket.

"You always were on your guard. Remember at the Sisters of Perpetual Help?"

"You're the reason why I smoke."

"I thought you said it was the Mother Superior?"

They laughed.

Odette elbowed Pet and she elbowed her back.

"So Sis, why've you come this time?"

"For advice."

"Ah, of course. Sometimes, my dear, and I mean no offense when I say this, but I think that they locked the wrong sister up."

"What do you mean?"

Odette wiped her mouth with her hand.

"Careful, darling, I'm only joking."

Pet clenched her coat closed. She looked around for an orderly. She was beginning to wish the nurse would come back.

"Don't worry, I passed dangerous a long time ago. I told you that they were about to let me out."

"Yes, darling, but that's what you always say."

"But this time I know it's for sure. But enough about me, what's going on with you?"

"We fought again. I don't think I can go on like this Odette."

"What do you mean, go on like this?"

"He's suffocating me."

"I'll kill him."

Pet got up. She looked out of the window.

"Don't say that Odette."

"It's just an expression."

"Don't even joke like that. They'll never let you out if they hear you talking like that."

"Oh they know me. They know I couldn't hurt a fly."

"Much."

"Sit back down, sister, and let us have a nice chat."

Pet sat back onto the bench. She leaned her head on Odette's shoulder. Odette pat her hair.

"Close your eyes. It's okay if you dose off, Pet. I'm here. I won't let anything harm you."

"I know," she said. "I always feel so safe around you, Odette."

"Yes, dear. We keep each other strong. You know it's your letters and phone calls that make it even bearable. I think about you and your life in New York and I fantasize what it must be like, you with your writer husband and your friends and your work. It keeps me going. It keeps me alive."

Pet turned and hit her head against the wall. She woke up. She was alone in the waiting foyer. She looked around for her sister. There was no one there. She heard keys jangling and listened as the nurse came down the hall carrying a tray. Pet brushed her hair and pushed it back and straightened her coat and skirt.

"Did I dream that? I couldn't have."

The nurse came through the doorway.

"I'm sorry it took so long but Lulu got out and we had a devil of a time getting her back into bed."

"Lulu?"

"Not serious, just demented," she chuckled.

"But aren't they all? Ha!"

She handed Pet a mug. It felt warm against her fingers.

123

"You're pale white. You look like you've seen a ghost."

Pet looked out over toward the window.

"What is it?"

Pet fumbled in her pocket for her cigarettes. She pulled a packet out.

"I'm sorry miss, we don't allow no smoking in here."

She pushed them back into her pocket. She wiped a drip of water off of her ear.

"You don't suppose that a resident could come through that doorway, do you?" The nurse leered.

"I know love, it gave me the creeps too when I first come here. But no, sweet, no one could get through them iron bars, unless they can walk through walls."

"It's not possible then?" She muttered to herself.

"What's that?"

She pulled a lipstick from her purse and quickly applied some around her lips.

"I have to go."

"But don't you want to see your sister," The nurse answered, a bit confused.

"Yes, but I have to check into the hotel and it is rather late and I don't want to wake her up."

"At least finish your café au lait."

Pet put the cup and saucer down on the bench and got up and straightened her coat.

"No really, you've been very kind but I've got to go. You see I had the most frightful dream while you were gone."

The nurse nodded.

"Don't surprise me in this place, all these yellings and screams. Not a place for a nice young lady like your self. You should just call us; I can give you the details. That's what the other families do." She fumbled with something in her pocket. "Just give me a minute to put these things away and I'll open the door for you."

The nurse picked up the tray and disappeared into the doorway. Pet listened as she dumped the dishes into a bin in the back. Pet thought she could hear shrill cries.

The nurse slowly came through the door and back into the foyer. It seemed to Pet that she was taking longer than usual to get the key to open the front door.

"Sadistic bitch," Pet thought.

The nurse opened the door. The moon was shining brightly onto the walk. The rain had stopped. She walked Pet to the gate, unlocked it and let her out.

"When can we be expecting you, I'll make a note in the log."

"I can't say when," she said as she hurried to the street and hailed a taxi.

124

"I'll call over once I've had a chance to get settled."

"As you wish, mum," the nurse replied.

Pet breathed a sigh of relief as she sat in the back of the taxi. She was wishing that Mont were there with her, protecting her. She thought about calling him, but gave the driver directions to her hotel instead, and then fell back into the seat, determined not to fall asleep until she was safely in her hotel room.

"I'll draw a hot bath and then call him. It is all so silly, really," she reassured herself.

Chapter Thirteen

"Hello, who is this?"

"It's Montgomery Clark, returning your phone call."

"Oh, hello Mr. Clark," Draza replied.

"Do you have any news for me?"

"Yes, Mont. is there a place where we can talk," she asked as she tried to untangle the telephone cord.

"I guess. There's a public park at 53rd street and Lexington Avenue. We can get a coffee there if it's convenient. I was at the library just jotting down a few ideas."

"Writing again?"

"In a manner of speaking, yes."

"Okay, I just have some paperwork to finish up here. Listen, we found a dead bird in your apartment, but it's missing."

"What?"

"I found a dead bird in your apartment, but it seems to be missing."

"Did he have a dab of red paint on his head," he asked curiously.

"Yes, how did you know?"

"I'll tell you all about it when I see you."

"I need ten minutes to finish up what I'm working on, then I can head out."

"I'll meet you in front of the coffee stand," Mont replied.

* * *

The Atrium at 53rd and Lexington Avenue was imposing. It was a courtyard area between two skyscrapers. In Manhattan Federal Tax Subsidies are given to buildings that provide a public park. This courtyard was one such place. The glass windows and steel girders, which outlined them, raised several stories high. Inside the atrium were metal grate type tables, chairs and petrified trees and plants.

Draza arrived carrying her briefcase and a file folder from Pet's case. She brushed through the door into the Atrium and walked over to the coffee stand. A grim looking worker forced a smile across his face and asked her what she wanted.

"Can you give me a second? Let me first look at the menu."

Her eyes scanned a sign above the man's head. There were several different variations of café, café au lait, café Americano, Skinny Latte, Vanilla Latte, and so on.

Draza pulled a twenty-dollar bill out of her coat pocket.

"Do you think you could manage a regular coffee and a buttered roll?"

"We have scones."

"Okay then just give me a coffee and a scone."

The man smiled. He poured the coffee into a paper cup and added milk and two sugars. He then grabbed a piece of wax paper and said, "which one."

"Any one," she answered, annoyed.

He grabbed the first one from the counter. It was a little crushed on the end.

She handed him the money and he gave her the change and forced another smile, along with her coffee and scone. She took the items and noticed as he tapped on a jar marked TIPS.

"Well you don't expect me to tip you for that! I mean I didn't get the roll."

"Please miss, we live on tips."

"Don't we all, more than you know," she said as she walked away from the counter.

Her eyes scanned the open space. There were quite a few tables inhabited by people who looked as though they might have slept there the night before. She found a table nearest the windows and beneath one of the faux poplars. Carefully she laid out her file, and placed her briefcase on a neighboring chair. As she sat a flutist came in and began playing lightly an English melody. Draza took a deep, cleansing breath. She took a sip of her coffee, smiled and closed her eyes.

A few minutes later she awoke as a man dragged a chair from the table. It was Mont. She wiped the soot from her eyes.

"I hope I'm not disturbing you?" He laughed.

"No," she replied, a bit embarrassed. "I was just resting my eyes."

Mont chuckled. He set his extra large coffee down on the table along with a folded Times.

She examined his cup.

"What'dya get?"

"Oh this" he said as his eyes glanced down to his coffee cup. "It's a Skinny Vanilla Latte."

"Any good?"

"Here," he said, smiling, "take a sip."

He pushed his cup toward her. She picked it up by the cardboard holder and sipped.

She put the cup down.

"Don't like it?"

"It's a little too sweet for my taste. I like my coffee to be coffee."

"Fair enough," Mont said.

"So what was it you had to tell me?"

"First let's get to you. Anything new transpire? The last I saw of you, you were en route to the Emergency Room. How's the head?"

Mont rubbed the back of his cranium.

"Doing nicely, I should say, at least where the bruises are concerned."

"That's good to hear. What took you so long to get back to me?"

Mont shuffled the newspaper on the table and looked over at a vagrant who was asleep and mumbling something.

"I've had rather an odd experience and, I don't know that I should tell you about it. I mean, you might think I've gone off it."

"Gone off what? What are you talking about?"

"I went the other day to see a psychic." He paused, turned the paper over, scanned the headline and looked up."

"You went to see a what?"

Mont rubbed his lip and took a sip of his latte. It was hot and nearly burned his lips. He put the coffee down.

"Actually she said that she was a," he paused and scratched his eyebrow, "Root Worker, whatever that is."

Draza hid a laugh in her cupped hand.

"And what did she tell you?"

"She had a lot of hokum going on. I'm not sure that I understand all of it." He rubbed his head. "And the thing about the bird. Now that really puzzles me."

Draza pushed some papers that had slid out back in to the file folder.

"Wait a minute. What bird? This Swami mentioned a bird?"

He chortled. "Well I wouldn't exactly call her a Swami. She's more like an elderly grandmother." He rubbed his eyebrow. "That's right, I think at one point that I thought she was my nanny."

"Don't you mean, 'mammy?'"

"That's not even funny. Draza, I'm surprised at you."

"I'm sorry Mont, it's just early in the morning and I haven't had my coffee."

"Isn't that what you're drinking?"

"I'm not sure what it is that I'm drinking."

She took a large gulp from her cup, put it down and wiped her mouth with her sleeve. She looked up at him, embarrassed, took up a paper napkin and then delicately dabbed her lips.

"Tell me about the bird."

"Okay, I'll try." He sipped his latte and swallowed and then made a noise as if to clear his throat. "You'll have to forgive me, I'm all congested. My allergies are acting up."

"Can't you take something for that?"

"I would but it gives me a foggy head, more than usual, and I need my thoughts to be clear when I'm writing."

"And are you writing?"

"Slowly, it's coming back."

"Go on. Just tell me about the bird."

"I don't know why it's so important to you, but anyway, when I was a boy," he motioned with his hand, holding it out to show that he was about three feet tall. She laughed. "I found a sparrow with a broken wing. I took him in and nursed him back to health and for awhile he seemed to be my only friend." He looked up at her. She sipped her coffee. "It was my first year at school. I was the new kid and you know how it goes, rite of passage and all that."

"I get it. Small boy, no friends, bird."

"Right. I had this pet bird. Eventually he got better and flew away, but I never forgot him."

"So how does this tie in?"

"Pam," he looked up, "that's the name of the root worker, "told me that my bird had crossed over from the other side,"

"Crossed over," she interrupted.

"River Styx or something, I don't remember my mythology, but apparently my bird came to protect me."

"That's funny."

Mont stared into her blue eyes. "Why is that peculiar?"

"We found a sparrow at your apartment in the top drawer of your bedroom bureau."

"You did. You never mentioned it to me."

"You mean you didn't know about it?"

"Of course not. What did you think, that I'm some nut that keeps dead birds in his apartment?"

"How am I supposed to know what you do in your apartment? We needed to make an investigation."

"So you think I keep dead birds in my apartment?"

"I've seen stranger."

"I bet you have," he said, annoyed. He turned to watch as a man rifled around a trash bin looking for cans.

"Tell me about your pet bird," Draza suggested.

"I dabbed him on the forehead with red paint and called him Jeremy."

Draza's face dropped.

"What is it?"

"This bird had red paint on its head."

"Can I see it?"

"No, he's missing."

"Missing?" Mont shuffled the paper and tapped his cup.

"Did the psychic tell you anything else about the bird?"

"Only that the werewolf had it."

Draza chuckled, "Oh she is a sly one. This root worker of yours."

"And why is that?"

"My last name is Slovakian for werewolf."

Draza's cell phone rang. She motioned with her index finger to Mont and then got up and walked away from the table. He could hear her speaking in hushed tones.

He sipped his coffee and read the paper. After a few moments, she returned to the table.

"Trouble?"

"Just my Uncle. It's Saturday."

"I remember…"

They laughed.

"Listen, can you take me over to this Root Worker?"

"Why?"

"The bird we found at your apartment has vanished. I want to get to the bottom of this."

"She said that would happen."

"And so where's the bird?"

"Pam said that he returned to the other side."

"Now I've heard everything."

"You mean you don't believe it?"

"There's a rational explanation for everything. Can you take me there now?"

"Okay. But don't you need a search warrant or something?"

"No, the first time is friendly. After that we bring in the big guns."

They got up from the table. Mont deposited his paper into a trash receptacle. Draza slipped the folder into her briefcase and they hurried out through a revolving door. Draza hailed a taxi and Mont directed the driver who took them up to the brownstone where Mont had met Pam.

As they pulled up to the building he noticed that the windows were all boarded up. They got out of the taxi. Draza looked over at the building.

"Are you sure that this is the place?"

The taxi spun away.

"Yes, I was just here the other day." He climbed the stairs to the building door. He rubbed his fingers over the doorbells. Rubbing the dusty front door pane he tried to peer into the foyer. Inside he saw broken plaster and garbage on the tiled floor.

Draza noticed a woman walking her dog. She stopped her.

"Miss, can I ask you a question?"

The woman looked up at Draza and over at Mont and smiled.

"No, Fitches, on the curb, remember what Mommy told you. We don't want to piddle on the flowers," she said to her Bichon Frise in a pink knit sweater as the dog attempted to pee on some flowers planted at the base of a tree. The woman looked up to speak with Draza as Fitches secretly squat down and relieved herself in the planter and then looked up at her owner to see if she'd been found out.

"Are you interested in buying the place," the woman asked.

Draza looked out toward the river and then back at the woman and nodded.

"I love it when a nice young couple like yourselves moves into the neighborhood. It's a good thing. And children's' laughter, I love to hear it. There's nothing like children playing in the park. Do you plan to have a lot of children and tell me, do you play the piano? I used to teach piano. I could maybe teach again."

"No. I mean, what can you tell me about the building."

"There used to be a real estate sign there." She looked up and down the building. I guess someone took it down. From what I hear," she tapped her lips with the dog's leash, "and this is just from the ladies at Hadassah, mind you…nosey old things, but what they tell me is that the owner died and the property's gone to probate. The

Relatives are fighting over it. But, sweetie, I'm sure a nice girl like you would have no trouble. Listen, my name is Rosie and I live just two doors over. Should you need anything, anything at all, you just come over and I'll see what we can do. You'd be surprised what a group of ladies can accomplish. You see these flowers here, we did this."

Rosie looked down at the planter. Fitches had deposited a nugget on the planter.

"Shame on you, Fitches! Now look what Mommy has to clean up!" Rosie pulled a piece of newspaper from her raincoat pocket, leaned over and scooped up the fecal matter and then deposited it into a nearby trash receptacle.

"I had one of those pooper scooper contraptions, but I never could figure out how to use it."

Draza shuffled her briefcase.

"There doesn't seem to be anyone in there." Mont called as he climbed down the stairs.

"Listen Sweetie, it looks like your husband needs you. Men, they're useless without us. I've got one at home. If I don't fix his lunch, he'd starve to death!"

"Thanks for your help."

"Listen, in this world where would we be without good neighbors!" She wrapped the leash around her wrist and tugged at the dog to move with her, as she walked on she said, "I meant it, what I told you about helping. You and husband, you'll talk, you'll see, we'll do. Okay, bye bye."

"Thanks, I appreciate it."

Rosie waved as she shuffled down the street to the end of the block. She had an odd little wobble as she moved. She turned the corner, the little dog trailing behind her wagging its tail. Mont jogged over to where Draza was standing.

"What was that all about?"

"Just doing a little research."

"The place looks like it's been abandoned. You don't think the root worker high-tailed it out of here?"

Draza examined her watch.

"I have an idea. How do you feel about having lunch with my Uncle Ignác?"

"You mean that colorful character from the precinct?"

"The very same."

"I'd love it."

"Okay, let's find the subway and I'll take you out there. It'll just be a simple lunch, but I'm sure none like you've ever had before."

"Oh I don't know about that."

"Exactly, you don't know about it," she smiled as she tugged on his blazer sleeve.

Chapter Fourteen

"Could you slow down? I've had rather a rough night," he said as he hurried to reach Draza who was dashing up the staircase from the Brighton Beach subway station, two steps at a time.

"No offense, but you don't know my Uncle Ignác."

"I'm sure he'll understand." Mont said, while trying to catch his breath.

They hurried from the subway to Ignác's apartment on Banner Avenue. Draza rang the bell and pushed the intercom button. She heard some arguing.

"No Irma, let me. It's my niece."

"But I need you to do what I told you…"

There were some muffled sounds. Irma got on to the speaker.

"I am just to release the door now, sweetie. You and your young gentleman friend can take the stairway. The elevator is not working so well. Mrs. Rosenblatt, you remember, the one with the kidney stones? She does her laundry on Saturdays and she's holding the lift up."

Within a few seconds a buzzer went off and a bell rang. Draza pulled open the door. Mont stood for a moment marveling at the old building. Draza pulled him in by his lapel.

"Mont I told you we were late."

"Okay, got it." He smiled boyishly.

Draza hurried up the steps once again with Mont at her heals.

"Linda Carter has nothing on you," he whispered between breaths.

"What?"

"Never mind, old television reference."

"Oh."

Irma opened the doorway and showed them in.

"You get the coats Iggy, and then fix them the drinks."

Uncle Ignác came in from a hallway. He was rubbing down his nearly bald scalp with his hand.

He motioned and took Draza's coat.

"Do you want for me to maybe hang up your wool jacket? It's a little hot in here from the oven," he said to Mont.

"No," Mont replied. "I think I'll keep it if you don't mind."

"Listen son, in my day a gentleman never removed his jacket in the presence of a lady. It was considered rude to be in your naked shirt sleeves."

"And what day was that Uncle? I thought you lived at The Battery?"

Irma rushed in from the kitchen. She was wearing a mustard floral apron. Smiling, she exposed a gold tooth. She took Draza's coat from Iggy and draped it over her arm.

"How nice you look today, Draza." She smiled.

Draza grinned back at her concealing a blush. Irma disappeared into the back bedroom with the coat.

"What would you have to drink? I have Corgon or Saris," Uncle Ignác interjected.

Mont looked over at Draza, grinning.

"You're going to have to help me out here, I have no idea what he just said."

"See, I told you." She poked him. "It's beer."

Mont looked around at the three-bedroom apartment. There was a balcony. The sliding glass doors just barely revealed the top corner of a roller coaster.

"You aren't far from the beach," Mont asked.

"It's a ten minute stroll." Uncle Ignác replied.

"Oh?"

"I know, why don't we crack open the bottle of the Slivovica," he chimed.

Uncle Ignác got up and went over to a bar, a 1950s style, made of blonde wood. Opening the top he produced a bottle. He pryed opened the cork and poured the beverage into two miniature wine glasses about one quarter full. He handed one towards Draza.

"None for me, I need to keep a clear head. I'll just have some Kofola." She leaned over and whispered, cola into Mont's ear.

"You'll have one, young man," Ignác asked.

"I can always use a drink," Mont replied. Mont held up the tiny wine glass to his nose and took a sniff. The fragrance of the plum-flavored wine filled his nostrils. He took a tiny sip.

Ignác pushed the cork back into the bottle and carried it in to the kitchen. He appeared a few seconds later carrying a glass of cola for Draza. Irma popped her head through a louvered pass through window.

"I'll just be a moment."

She came out of the kitchen a few seconds later also carrying a small glass of cola. She took her apron off and wiped her forehead with a napkin.

"It's very hot in there. I keep telling Ignác that he should get a new exhaust fan."

"This one, she's always spending like it's hers to do with," he answered.

"Now for me, I have a nice new kitchen. I had it put in by my son-in-law, Sol. He does kitchens for cheap. I have the stainless. It's nice. Hard to keep clean with this one." She nudged Ignác who sat close to her on the chair. "He gets his hands on everything."

"Not everything," he joked.

"Come, sit around the table and I'll bring out the soup." Irma disappeared into the kitchen.

"You'd have loved it back in the old country."

"What, Battery Park," Draza remarked.

"No, that was different. Before they built the skyscrapers. We all lived down there and on weekends we played stickball, had dances and temple."

"And then he moved out here."

"We all moved. They wouldn't let us stay in the…what's the word, Draza?"

"Tenement, Uncle Ignác."

"Right, they made us move. But I had more room and the ocean and it was good for the baby."

"Me," Draza said as she thumbed her chest.

"I raised her. Her father," he looked over at Draza as they moved to the dining room area table, "you don't mind if I tell him?"

"Could I stop you?"

He laughed.

"Her parents died. Her father (he held his hand to his heart), the war, her mother (he waved his hands in the air), ballet."

"Ballet killed your mother," Mont asked as he looked for a chair.

"You'll have to sit on the stool. It's a tradition," she said.

Mont found a chair that was also part step stool. It had steps that folded underneath.

"Now I bet you haven't done that before?" Uncle Ignác added.

"Not true, cook had one of these in the kitchen. I think I remember. I did sit on one once."

"It's just that there was a party and…"

"No need to explain. I'm fine with the stool." Mont sat down. He was about two inches higher than everyone else at the table.

Irma came into the room carrying a tray with bowls of soup and a plate of rye bread. She handed each of them a steaming bowl and then dashed in and out of the kitchen and returned a few times until all of the food was on the table. Ignác got up and pulled out a chair for her and then they all sat down to eat. Mont examined his soup.

"What is this again?"

"I don't think we said," Ignác replied, "it's Kapustnica."

"Kapoostee-what?" He stabbed at it with his spoon.

"I think maybe Draza can help us with the translation."

"Oh I love a good Kapustica," she laughed.

"Are you going to tell me what's in here," Mont said as he swirled his spoon around the bowl picking at leafy greens that floated in the murky mixture.

"Sure, it's cabbage, pork sausage and…" she looked over at Irma. Irma pulled her in toward her and whispered into her ear. "and plums."

"Let's join hands," Ignác said. "Will you say the blessing, Draza?"

Draza uttered a prayer in Yiddish.

They all looked up. Ignác smiled and they began dipping their spoons into the soup and slurping it down. Mont laughed, took a mouthful and slurped loudly with them.

"This is good. You'll have to give me the recipe."

"Not the chance," Irma replied. "This goes with me to the grave." She looked up thinking, and then over at Mont. "Unless it's for a wedding present."

"You'll have to forgive them, Mont. They aren't used to company."

"Since when do you have boys around," Irma replied.

"He's a client." Draza remarked.

"Client she says, Iggy." She nudged his elbow. "And clients can't be husbands?"

"Enough now, Irma. She's a grown woman. She knows her mind."

"Thanks, papa." Draza whispered.

Not knowing what to say or do, Mont dipped some buttered rye bread into the froth and took a bite.

After supper Irma busily cleared away the dishes. Mont went to button his blazer and the top button came out in his hand.

"Darn. I knew that was going happen. I've been wearing this jacket entirely too much."

"Give it to me." Draza said.

He looked up, bewildered.

"Just hand it over preppie. Irma, can you give me a hand with this?"

Irma popped her head through the window.

"I have some thread and the needle in my apartment. Come with me dear," she said.

The two women left. The front door slammed behind them.

"Come out to the balcony and have a smoke."

"How did you know I smoke?"

"A smoker can always tell another smoker."

Ignác pulled out a cigar from his jacket pocket and slid open the sliding glass doors.

"You have trouble," he said as he lit up his cigar. He handed a cigar to Mont who promptly clipped off the tip with the clipper Ignác handed him and took a light from Ignác's match which was waving, about to burn his fingers. Ignác blew out the match and tossed it from the balcony.

"I don't know that I should tell you."

"Please, we are friends here."

"Okay. I went to see this old woman, a psychic. She told me that I was in danger and that someone was out to kill me. She was an odd sort. When I went to the building this morning with Draza, it was boarded up and it seemed as though no one had been there for some time."

"And the address you had, it was correct?"

"Yes. It's an unusual building. There is a view of the river. I wouldn't forget it. We writers pay close attention to detail."

Ignác took a long drag of his cigar, exhaled and tapped it out the window. They stood on the balcony for several moments smoking. After awhile Ignác put out his cigar and Mont followed suit. Ignác took the butt from Mont and they went inside. Mont could hear Draza and Irma talking as they did the dishes in the kitchen.

Ignác produced two bottles of Corgon beer from a mini fridge in the bar. He opened them and handed one to Mont.

"Can I ask you what you think?"

"First drink some beer, and then I'll tell you."

Mont drank a few sips of beer and Ignác began speaking.

"When I was young we had this woman. She came to us when there was danger. Some say she came because we used the Golem. Other's say she was someone's relative. But she always would come and warn us. I think maybe your woman is such a person."

"So you think she's a person?"

"Not really. I have to find the words. Give me a moment."

They sat back drinking. Ignác cleared his throat.

"She was a guide."

"Oh like a spiritual guide."

"Yes."

"And what about the building?"

"I have lived in this city for many years. Longer than any place else." He put his beer down on a cardboard Coney Island coaster.

"There are portals in New York that lead to other times. When I first came to New York with Draza's Aunt Minnie, we stayed in The Chelsea Hotel. It was for a kind of Honeymoon, one we never had when we were married. But I had a good job; import/export and I promised her that we'd have a few nights in a fancy hotel. She wanted the kitchen and balcony and so we stayed there."

"That sounds nice. I've heard of the place, musicians, writers, etc."

"I thought you'd like this story."

"Go on."

"I woke in the middle of the night. We had a *Husacie Hody* of sorts, not like at Slovensky Grob, but as close as you can find in America, and I was feeling a bit of indigestion. I couldn't find the Bramo seltzer, so I got up and left the room. I thought maybe I'd go downstairs and find the druggist open."

"So what's so unusual about that?"

Ignác grabbed his shoulder and pulled him close.

"You will think that this is just an old man talking, but believe me when I tell you, once I left that room, I was not in this time."

Mont pulled his arm off his sleeve and sat back. He looked around the room; it was crowded with antique furniture and framed pictures of what appeared to be family members.

"I don't follow you."

"I saw men in top hats and women in bustles. As I climbed down the stairs and looked out the front door onto West 23rd street there were dirt roads, and horses with carriages. The air tasted differently. The city had lost the buzz I remembered. I stood for the moment and pinched myself. I could not believe it. But there I was, in my nightclothes, standing on the street. I felt something beneath my bare foot. I picked it up. It was a skeleton key from the last century. I put it in my pocket. I ran up to my room opened the door. Locked it behind me and got in to bed with my wife. The next day I told her."

"And what did she say?"

"We laughed. She said that I had too much to drink and that I'd imagined it all."

"And did you?"

"I thought so. But then I felt something in my pocket." He reached into his pocket.

"It was the key."

"You got it?"

"So let me get this straight. You are saying that there are doorways that lead to other times?"

"All over the city," he said as he waved his hands about.

"And so what I did was travel back in time?"

"I don't think we can travel forward, so much as I've been able to find."

"So when I opened the door of the brownstone with the psychic, I walked back into the 1970s?" Mont asked.

"Wait, did you touch the door?"

"No. It was open."

"That's what I'm a talking about."

Draza entered the room holding Mont's blazer.

"What are you two doing? Not getting up to any troubles are you?"

"No, I was just telling your nice young man about The Chelsea Hotel."

Draza handed the repaired jacket to Mont.

"Oh, Uncle Ignác, not that story again." She looked over at Mont. "He was hung-over."

"And the key? How do you explain that, Draza?"

"He could've found that anywhere? Maybe he actually did step on it. But even Aunt Minnie, may she rest in peace (she said as she tapped her lips with her hand and held it up to the ceiling), said that he was sleep walking. He did that a lot in those days.

Ignác waved his hand at Draza. "This young generation, they don't believe anything."

"We should get going." Draza leaned over and kissed her uncle on the head.

They got up from the table. Mont put on his jacket and they headed for the door.

"It was very nice to meet you young man."

"Thank you, sir. But I bet you say that to all the boys."

"What boys? You're the first Draza has ever brought here." He smiled.

Mont rubbed his mouth. He shook the man's hand and then went out the door. Irma called after him, "It was nice to meet you, Montgomery. Don't be the stranger. Come again, we'll go to the beach and you and Draza can do the rides. It's quite the few from the Ferris."

"Yes'm," he replied.

Mont slowly stepped down the stairs a little woozy from the drink.

As she made her way through the front door, Uncle Ignác stopped her from behind. He held Draza by the shoulders for a moment and then handed her a religious item.

"What's this for?"

"Listen, Draza, you are like the daughter to me. Ever since your mother died and your Aunt Minnie, you're all I have in the world. Please, make an old man happy and hang this over your entry."

"Why?"

"This boy, he's nice. Not Slovak, but nice. But he's not for you. He finds himself dancing with the Devil, Draza. He saw the woman, the guide, like Ida Bertelsman."

"Listen Uncle, what happened to her is not going to happen to him or to me. That was a coincidence."

"You and your flukes. Take it," he said as he handed it to her. She put it into her bag and kissed him on the cheek.

"Now let me go."

"He's nice." Irma came in smiling. She pulled Ignác away from the door. Come on Iggy, let's have a nice game of cards and let these two young people to their business. Your Uncle Draza is such a work, but what man isn't," she joked. Ignác closed the door behind Draza. She climbed down the stairs and outside where she found Mont.

Mont stood quietly smoking a Gitanes.

"So what's the verdict?" She mused.

"The verdict is," he said as he flicked his cigarette to the curb, "that you were right, I haven't ever experienced anything like that before."

"They're strange, stuck to their old ways, I know."

"That's not what I was talking about. Your family is very close. It was nice. I never had that growing up."

"We have to walk this way," she said, "to the B express."

"And how long does it take us to get back into Manhattan?"

"You, you mean. I live out here."

"Right, how long?"

"It's about 35 minutes into Manhattan."

"Oh."

"But before you go, I wanted to give you this."

"What?"

Draza pulled a flyer from her pocket. She handed it to Mont.

"What is this," he asked as he quickly.

"A parting gift," she said.

Mont scanned the notice. "DETTE PRESENTS: Les Décès et Les Disparitions, an art exhibit at La Gallerié de Bécassine (LP), Grand opening Sunday, November 3rd, 6-8pm featuring the artwork of Petula Beaujolais-Clark.

"I found her through an odd coincidence. Apparently there were a series of accidental deaths connected with the art show. And it seems her best friend, Sophie is now missing."

"Who died?"

"The art handler was in an accident while he was transporting the pieces from her studio. That's where she'd been living, on 17th street. And the publicist had an allergic reaction to something he ate. And there was one other…"

Draza realized that she'd lost his attention. She looked over at a passing ice cream truck. It's melody eerily played into the night.

"I didn't know she still had that studio," he said as his mind trailed, "and where is this show?"

"In a section of Manhattan known as 'Little Paris.' It's just below Eighth Street on the lower eastside.

"Did you speak to her?"

"Your wife? Yes. I had a long conversation with her. She doesn't want to see you again, Mont. She said that it's over."

Mont rubbed his eyes and took a deep breath. He leaned against the building for a moment. He looked up at Draza who seemed concerned.

"No, I'm alright. I expected as much. I just feel a little queasy from the sweet wine and the beer."

"Do you want me to take you home? I have a pink Vespa in a garage not far from here."

"You have a what?"

"It's a long story for another time. I just wanted to let you know that the Sergeant says your case is finished. Petula is no longer a missing case; in fact she's giving an art show. But really, Mont, she doesn't want to see you. Maybe you shouldn't go there."

"How can you say that, when you know I have to? I need to confront her. I need some closure."

He took a deep breath. He could taste salt in the air and smell the sea.

"This was nice," she said as she traced the outline of some red bricks on the building and called his attention back to herself.

"It was," he said, smiling. "I'll call you."

He tapped her on the shoulder.

"Seriously," he reassured her.

She buttoned her coat, turned up the collar and watched as he jogged down the street toward the subway station. He nearly stumbled down the stairs. Quickly, he slid his Metro card and then pushed through the turn-style just in time to slip between the closing doors of the subway train, its chime bleeped twice, the doors closed and the train pulled out of the station.

Chapter Fifteen

The B train into Manhattan seemed to take an eternity to get across the river and on to the island. Mont counted the stops. The train was empty. It rattled back and forth. As it pulled into the station Mont spotted the words, "Love Never Dies" spray-painted on one of the tunnel walls. He stood up and waited in front of the subway doors until they opened. As he approached the platform a woman stood with a microphone in her hand. Beside her was a poster with the words, REPENT, THE KINGDOM OF GOD IS AT HAND. He stopped and listened to her for a moment as she boomed out in a hell and brimstone pitch, looking directly at Mont, "I am convinced, child, that neither death nor life, child, neither angels nor demons," she waved her Bible in the air, "neither the present nor the future, nor any powers," she pat on her Bible, "neither height nor depth, nor anything else in ahhhhhhl creeaaaashun, will be able to separate us from the LOVE OF GOD…" she put the Bible down on a stand and tapped a tambourine at her side, "can I get an Amen up in here?"

Mont reached into his pocket and pulled out a five-dollar bill. He handed it to the woman.

"Bless you child. It will come back to you seven fold."

Mont hurried up the stairs and bolted from the station. He hailed a taxicab in front of The Waverly Diner.

"Where can I take you, bub?" A greasy man in a newsboy hat called from the front seat.

"You don't happen to know where Little Paris is? I'm trying to get to a gallery, Miss Clark, or rather, Ms. Beaujolais, an artist."

"You're just in luck. I took some tourists down there. Funny, now they're calling it Little Paris. You're too young to know this, but we had a guy, artist who had a gallery there back in the 60s. I gave him a ride then. He was a farmer, or the son of one- Andy Warhol. Heard of him?"

Mont smiled at the driver as the car raced passed throngs of tourists in the village streets. The car pulled up in front of an old warehouse that had been converted into a gallery. A large flag dangled with the name, Petula Beaujolais stitched vertically.

"This it?"

"Yes. Thank you."

Mont swiped his credit card down the side of the machine and tapped in a tip. He hurried from the taxi and climbed the stairs up to the gallery. He was anxious to see his wife.

Two large men in blue suits blocked his entry. One stepped forward and put his hand up against Mont's chest.

"I'm sorry, Sir, but the gallery is not open. The show is tomorrow and will go on through November."

Mont tried to push his way past the man and in to the gallery. "This is my wife's show."

The large man looked to his partner. "The Countess never mentioned she was married. D'ya think he's fronting?"

The other guard shrugged his shoulders.

The guard shoved Mont and he fell backward to the floor. A slight figure came just then appeared through the doors and in to the anterior of the structure.

"What is going on here," she probed.

"Uh, Ms. Beaujolais, this man tried to get in to the gallery. We told him it wasn't open but he persisted."

"And this is how you treat our patrons, by throwing them to the floor? Step back," she commanded. She pressed the guard to the side.

"Leave this to me."

"I was just trying to do my job." The guard muttered as he walked in to the back room with the other guard.

The woman extended her hand to Mont. He looked up. Her hair was blonde and short. Her face was identical to his wife. She pulled him up and he stood, marveling at her similarity to Petula.

"Do I know you," he asked.

"Who are you?"

"I am Montgomery Clark. This is, I believe, my wife's art show."

"Ah yes. I was expecting you. Will you come with me please, Mr. Clark?"

Mont followed her into the gallery. He looked everywhere at the artwork, some of which was still being hung on the walls that surrounded them. The art was enormous and garish.

"She specialized in Fauvism. See the bright colors. It reminds me a bit of Matisse. And be careful of the sculptures."

"I had no idea…"

"She did a study of all the art forms. Apparently one must do this to get the degree in Fine Arts."

"And who are you," Mont asked.

She directed him into a small kitchen area.

"Would you like some coffee? I brought it with me from Paris."

Mont nodded. He looked out at the gallery. There were several paintings of a figure that he thought might be of him.

The woman poured him a cup of coffee and one for herself from a French press and motioned for him to sit down directly across from her.

They sat down.

He noticed something odd about her. Her walk and manner seemed a bit masculine. And the way she held her cup, a tight grip on the stoneware handle. She extended her hand.

"Allow me to introduce myself, I am Odette Beaujolais. But you may call me "Dette.""

He shook her hand. Her grip crunched his fingers and made them sting.

"Ah, now it makes sense. You are her sister. You're her twin? Right?"

"Yes, I was her twin."

"Was?"

"I don't know how to tell you this, Monsieur Clark, but perhaps it's better this way, coming from family."

"What is it?"

"My sister," she paused and circled her index finger in the hole of her cup and then all at once said, "my sister is dead, she expired in my arms. When she left you that night, she came to me."

Mont put his cup down. He looked at her closely. She cupped her eyes with her hand. He took a deep breath.

"So she flew to France that night. No wonder I couldn't find her."

He was in shock. He didn't know what he was feeling. He seemed not to feel anything at all. Not knowing what else to say, he asked, "And where is she now?"

"I have her ashes with me back at the studio."

"I'm puzzled. I was told that she was alive. A detective told me."

"Ah yes, Ms. Vicaru." She took a sip of her coffee and swallowed hard.

She looked up at Mont.

"I never told her that I was Petula. I told her that I was Ms. Beaujolais. Besides, it was easier for people to believe that I was my sister. After all, I'm only doing what she asked."

Mont rubbed his lip.

"What do you mean? I'm confused."

"It's funny about sisters. Did she ever tell you about when we were little girls, what happened?"

"No, not really. She just said that you were in Clarenton."

"We were on the see-saw. We had to be about eight years old. A boy, Jacques, something or other, took her doll. She jumped from the ride to chase after him. That was when I fell. I hit my head. I was knocked unconscious and needed stitches. You can still see the scars."

"That's unfortunate."

"It is," she said as she rubbed her forehead. "But it's a good thing, because they took me to the hospital and after that they put me in Clarenton where I have lived for most of my life."

"I was aware, but she never went in to too much detail."

"I feel as if I know you, Mr. Clark. She sent me letters every week and telephone calls. You'll forgive if I'm candid?"

"No, please, go ahead. This interests me." He took a sip of his coffee and stared into her eyes. How much they were like Pet's, he thought.

"I hated you, Mr. Clark. I felt like you were killing her."

"There was a note…" he interrupted.

"Oh, sorry about that."

"The note?"

"I didn't write the note."

"Then who did?"

"Of that I cannot be sure. There are many things going on that I don't quite understand, like the blasted deaths, as if I had anything at all to do with them. But I needed that painting for the exhibit and the key I had didn't work in the lock."

"There's a trick to it," he said. He tapped the outside of his mug.

"And the deaths, they were accidental," he added.

"What can I tell you? The weak ones die, the strong ones thrive," she said, matter-of-factly as if she were talking about the weather. Mont put his hand down on his knee.

"How did my wife die? Was there any pain?"

He pushed the coffee cup away from him on the table. He peered out into the gallery space. His nerves were jumping like little pins. His glance moved from painting to painting – the vibrant faces seemed to call out to him.

"There was no pain. She was visiting me. I was about to be released having been cured. It's amazing what they can do with all the new drugs. I'd been, 'stabilized.' She was visiting when she suddenly had an attack."

'Dette took a sip of her coffee.

"Attack?"

'Dette smiled and picked up a napkin and wiped her mouth. "There were complications of the heart. Surely you knew this, it was hereditary?"

"I don't remember," he said, "there might have been something."

"Something, he says." She turned her face from him for a moment to hide her expression of disgust. She looked back at him squarely.

"She perished in my arms."

Mont turned away. He felt a tear trickle down his cheek. He wasn't aware that he'd started crying. He wiped it with his fist.

"I hated you, Mr. Clark. I blamed you for robbing her of her life. She was an artist, but it seemed as though you usurped her. Once I got here to the states, I found her diary at her artist studio. I read about you and her and your life together, I hope you don't mind, but I had to know."

"No. It's okay, you're her sister."

"And when I saw how much she loved you, I decided to pardon you from any blame."

"And you came here, why?"

"She asked me to do this." Odette wiped her eyelash. "It was her dying wish."

"This," he said as he waved his hand about the gallery.

"The art show," she replied flatly. "Petula asked me to put her in a gallery and show off her work. An artist is immortal so long as her work lives on in the hearts and minds of others."

"Ah, I see," he said.

"Do you really?" She picked up her cup and brought it over to the sink. She turned on the water and rinsed it out poking with her fingernail at imaginary grains of sugar.

"Tell me Mr. Clark, do you have any idea what it's like to be an identical twin?"

"I had a twin, but he died before we were born. So I guess I do and I don't. I always feel like a part of me is missing. It's as if I was in another room somewhere, in another dimension, and yet here at the same time."

"It's awful not having her here. I finally get out of the Looney bin. We had such plans. We were going to tour with her art around the world together. And now she's gone. Life is such a thief!"

"You never get it all," he said, dryly.

"Come, I've so much to do before we open tomorrow." She came to the table and as he stood up added,

"And if there's anything I can do, you'll let me know." Mont felt as if he'd been dismissed. He felt tightness in his throat.

"But of course. I hope we can be friends." She smiled coyly, as if she'd rehearsed this entire speech. "I mean that. It's much harder for me than you know. I put on a stoic front, but inside, Mr. Clark, I'm all at sea."

"I know just what you mean," he said, "I've been walking in a daze for months. I feel I've only just woken up."

She followed as he walked down the stairs and to the front door. She trailed him as he stepped outside. Suddenly there was a loud metal squeak that sounded almost like the kind of shriek a child or a ghost would make. He looked up; it was a pulley above his head. He moved forward down the stairs and stood on the sidewalk in front of the building. The object being raised to the window on the second floor was of a large marble sculpture of birds and in the middle there seemed to be a carving of Montgomery's face. He watched as the men maneuvered it upward. 'Dette came down the front staircase and stood outside a few feet away from Mont on the sidewalk. She looked up at the sculpture. For a minute she held her hand on her cheek. And then Mont spotted it. On her wrist, there, in the smallest and most delicate of ways, painted with a heated pen, he saw the rose tattoo. Suddenly a million memories came flashing back to him of a summer holiday he and Petula took in Cape May. They'd gone on a day trip up to Wildwood and walked along

146

the boardwalk. Mont was against tattoos, but he and Pet went in to the parlor and both had matching rose tattoos made. His was above his heart. Her tattoo was on her wrist.

He turned towards 'Dette.

"What have you done to her?"

"What are you talking about?"

"I know you are not 'Dette. I know that you are Petula. What have you done with my wife?"

"Listen, it's best if you go. I release you."

"You don't have the power."

"She was weak. I had to get out of that place. Look at what I'm doing for her! She will be remembered forever. She is immortal."

"I'm not leaving."

"You must."

Mont looked up at the marble artwork. The pulley was caught.

"Is that meant for me? Are you going to kill me too, like you did the others?"

"Killing is such a violent word. No one took their lives."

"I am not weak and I am not going."

"You have to leave or depart this life."

"I'm not going. Do you want to know what love is? Dette, this is love, here right now. Love never dies. I'm standing here, and if it means that my life ends, so be it. Petula will know that my love is true. And I cannot be shaken or moved."

"As your will so mote it be," she said. She waved her hand in the air.

The fasteners, which attached the pulley, broke loose and the sculpture began to fall. Mont closed his eyes. At the last moment, a split second before it came crashing down, suddenly from the her mouth she screamed, "Montgomery! No! I will not..."

She ran into him and pushed against his body with the force of ten men. He went flying through the air and out of the way of the tumbling art. He crashed backward on to the concrete sidewalk about ten feet from her. She let out almost an animal sounding howl as the sculpture landed on top and crushed her. A crowd formed around them as her blood raced in streams to the curb.

Mont lost consciousness while the sound of sirens whirled over him like lullabies in his head.

Chapter Sixteen

The phone bell sounded deafening as it rang repeatedly into the darkness of the room. Mont reached over from his bed on to the nightstand and picked up the Bakelite receiver.

"Who is this?" He looked at the clock. It was 4 o'clock.

"Mont, is that you?"

"Bea, what are you calling me at four o'clock for?"

"Oh I'm sorry, darling, its ten o'clock here in Rome."

"You're still in Rome?"

"Well I had to call you to see how you are doing. I heard about the accident. Is every thing alright?"

"You're asking me this at four in the morning?"

He sat up in bed and wiped his eyes. Pressing the receiver against his face, he said, "It's not Bea, but it will be. We just had the funerals last week."

"Funerals?"

"Yes. Mother handled everything. I buried Petula in the family plot and took the urn and had it placed above ground in the plot by her side."

"So sad, Mont, both girls."

"Yes it was. But somehow I feel better Bea; just knowing they're up there in Sleepy Hollow, safe. Do you know what I mean?"

"It's the business of living, darling, people die every day. Sometimes it's people we love."

"People we love," he whispered to himself. He fumbled with a St. Christopher medal he had hanging from a chain around his neck.

"Say, Bea, what about you? What gives? You just tore off to Rome?"

"Had to, darling, Pam."

"Oh don't get me started on that cook. Is she for real?"

"Wait until you get an invoice from Pamela's House of Weaves for $2,500. Then you'll see how truly real she is."

"So you went to Rome without me? Are you coming back?"

"It's complicated."

"Oh Bea, I know that tone," he said as he switched on the light, "what's his name?"

"Believe it or not, darling, his name is Emilio, and he's a gondolier."

"Really, I find that hard to believe. Bea with someone in *service*?"

"You're not going to believe this, but I took your advice."

"You mean he isn't twenty years older?"

"He's twenty-eight, so just a few years younger than I am."

"In which lifetime, Bea?" He laughed.

"Don't be cheeky, Mont. Listen the reason why I called you was to let you know about Peter."

148

"Peter?"

"Yes. He's alive; Mont. He's been at Phelps Hospital all this time. Apparently when his car went in to the river he escaped and swam to shore. He hit his head or something, but they expect a full recovery."

"How'd you find out, Bea?"

"His people called my people. He was going to call you directly, Mont, but he thought that it might be too much of a shock, given the present circumstances."

"Oh, I see. Well that's good to hear. I'll have to get up there."

"Listen, Darling, I have to go, I'm having breakfast on the terrace at the Forum Hotel. It's too divine sitting out here above the rooftops of Rome. You'd love it. But the waiter is standing here ready to take my order and I'm meeting Emilio later. Hold on a moment…"

Mont listened as he heard her say, over-dramatically to the waiter, "*Cameriere, per favore portami uova benedetto, una mimosa e un bicchiere d'acqua. Pronto!*"

"Listen, darling, I'm going to ride this thing out for as long as it lasts, but let's get together for a nice long lunch at 21 when I return, okay, darling?"

"All right, Bea," he said.

Bea made a kissing sound in to the phone. Mont smiled and put the receiver back into the cradle; he turned out the light, slid down into the bed and pulled the covers up over his head.

www.ingramcontent.com/pod-product-compliance
Lightning Source LLC
Chambersburg PA
CBHW071305130626
46556CB00003B/1469